ACPL ITEM
DISCARDED

YO-BSM-416

The Shimmering Maya and Other Essays

The Shimmering Maya and Other Essays

By Catharine Savage Brosman

Louisiana State University Press — Baton Rouge and London

Copyright © 1994 by Louisiana State University Press
All rights reserved
Manufactured in the United States of America
First printing
03 02 01 00 99 98 97 96 95 94   5 4 3 2 1

Designer: Glynnis Phoebe
Typeface: text, Bembo; display, Park Avenue
Typesetter: G&S Typesetters, Inc.
Printer and binder: Thomson-Shore, Inc.

Library of Congress Cataloging-in-Publication Data
Brosman, Catharine Savage, 1934–
    The shimmering Maya, and other essays / by Catharine Savage
Brosman.
        p.   cm.
    ISBN 0-8071-1874-5 (cl)
    I. Title.
PS3552.R666S54   1994
814'.54—dc20   94-6065
                                                        CIP

"On Husbandry" was first published in *Sewanee Review,* XCIX (Spring, 1991), copyright
1991 by Catharine Savage Brosman. "Desert Silvery Blue" was first published in *Sewanee
Review,* C (Summer, 1992), copyright 1992 by Catharine Savage Brosman. "Prospecting"
was first published in *Sewanee Review,* CI (Spring, 1993), copyright 1993 by Catharine
Savage Brosman. "The Shimmering Maya: A Trip to Texas" and "Leaving for Good"
first appeared in *Southern Review.*

The paper in this book meets the guidelines for permanence and durability of the Com-
mittee on Production Guidelines for Book Longevity of the Council on Library Resources. ∞

For Kate

Contents

The Shimmering Maya and Other Essays

The Shimmering Maya: A Trip to Texas

*A*re there moments in everyone's life of yielding to the dream and believing that displacements are, by themselves, propitious? Perhaps this variety of *bovarysme* is not universal, but certainly some minds seem never to cease visualizing greener grass over every rise, that is, being fascinated by the shimmering Maya, that personification of illusion in Hindu philosophy. My father, a good man, devoted to his family, but neurotic, was inclined to this turn of mind, although he would not have admitted so for fear of encouraging it in me. (I did not require encouragement.) In what ways he had put this inclination to the test as a young man, and with what results, I do not know, except that he took some years more than the usual four to finish college, and more than one campus was involved. The penchant erupted often enough later for me to remember him as always ready to pull up stakes and move on. One long trip in particular remains memorable. To say that it took place under gas rationing is to evoke one of the myths (or, in Roland Barthes's term, mythologies) of this century, since, retrospectively, a whole complex of regrets, memories, political ideals, and monolithic moral judgments and a considerable iconographic code are tied to World War II and those years when gasoline, like sugar, coffee, meat, shoes, and other commodities, was strictly controlled. The need for gasoline was determined not by the number of family members but by use of the automobile for one's livelihood. My father, who had never become the dentist that his own father wished for him to be, had exercised, or would, a number of other professions and trades—grocer, high school teacher, driver's license examiner, newspaperman, camp director, census taker (1950), motel clerk, university professor (he even taught one year under the auspices of Oxford); he was then teaching at North High School in Denver, a position that certainly did not warrant extra gasoline. But somehow, although he was upright and would not have practiced misrepresentation, he had managed to get a ration sticker—a green decal affixed to the windshield—that would allow us to buy enough fuel to make the long drive from Colorado to Texas, eventually as far as the southernmost tip. We drove very slowly, keeping to the speed limit of thirty-five miles per hour, I believe—a law enacted chiefly to save wear on tires. With frequent stops, it took ten days.

. It was August, 1944. The United States had been involved in the war for more than two-and-a-half years. There had been shortages of meat and butter; we had spread on biscuits a white lardlike substance packaged in cellophane that could be colored by kneading in capsules of orange dye; we had had blackouts, and squadrons of bombers drummed through the skies. Our neighbors, more adept at such than my father, had victory gardens, and in the schools we collected tinfoil and cans and were regularly solicited to buy savings stamps, for a dime or quarter, that one pasted in a booklet and could apply to a twenty-five-dollar bond—later to be a victim of inflation. My uncle's wife regularly sent packages of coffee and sugar to her relatives in London and Belfast, and we in the Girl Scouts had prepared kits of soap, toothpaste, and such to be distributed to refugee children in Europe—a pitiful, derisory gesture, it now appears, in the face of the torture and murder of millions. The streetcars and public billboards carried posters showing variously the three tyrants, Uncle Sam, "V for Victory," and warnings that loose speech could endanger the lives of American soldiers. My father's brother Jack, having failed at a legal career during the Depression because the only clients he really cared to take were those who could not pay, had joined the navy and was somewhere in the Pacific. My cousin Beth Bradshaw, a nurse and an officer, was with Omar Bradley's army in Europe; they called each other "Brad." When my father opened the *Rocky Mountain News* one day in June 1944, he saw Beth pictured on the front page, with the first group of medical officers to land on the beaches. (When she returned from France at the war's end she brought me a silk handkerchief with the cathedral of Rheims and the date "May 8, 1945" embroidered in blue; it materialized for me a patriotism—I do not want to say chauvinism—that I un-

2

derstood imperfectly but had been transmitted by radio to my ears, and perhaps my heart, by the booming voice of Charles de Gaulle.) My uncle Kenneth was serving as an army doctor, and my cousins Raymond and John were stationed stateside. Yet, despite the constant talk of the war, I, at ten the youngest of the cousins, was still in a state of innocence, which to some degree matched, despite the conflict, the nation's own.

It was fallacious, to be sure. Children are ferocious and Arcadia is but a poet's dream, though an appealing one. Clearly, however, some periods are less violent and inhumane than others and carry—sometimes for themselves (as in the 1920s), sometimes only for historians—a cachet of exuberance, or share a vision of human possibility like that to which we owe the beginnings of our republic. Even if under the gilt of the Edwardian era, for instance, we now see large-scale injustice, exploitation, a robber-baron mentality, and the incipient colonial conflicts and ethnic rivalries that would lead to war, the decades before World War I lent some justification to the term *la Belle Epoque,* with what Modrus Eksteins calls its "brilliant though crepuscular atmosphere," whereas no one would think of applying the term to the 1930s. To suggest now that the years of the second world conflict were somehow a happy time, amid the destruction and terror, would seem to be yielding to the worst delusions of nostalgia, illustrated now in the fashion for "retro" music, movies, and airplanes of the 1940s. But there is a sense in which this mythology has value, as historians and the popular imagination alike have recognized. Compared to its conclusion—the atomic bombs dropped on Japan, which raised the killing to the level of even vaster massacres of civilians than those achieved by Bomber Command over Dresden and other German cities—earlier months of the war seemed humanly acceptable, partly because of the well-drawn lines between the good and the evil sides, which were blurred at the war's end and have been far less neat in subsequent conflicts, and also because much of the destruction, as a very slanted journalism revealed it to us, remained on the same scale of the individual that had been the measure in earlier conflicts—one soldier wounded in the fighting in North Africa or Italy, one fighter plane shot down, hostages executed in a French village in retaliation for resistance activities. In addition, postwar revelations concerning the concentration camps, about which, even in Europe, the average citizen had known little (Simone de Beauvoir, for instance, wrote that she was "far from suspecting" the real truth of the camps), made it clear in retrospect that the period had been one of unprecedented crimes against helpless millions, which cast on the past and the future alike the shadow of utter human depravity. In that shadow a number of us finished growing up.

My parents' choice to leave Denver and head south—without any plan at all—was made when, in midsummer, my father, whose lungs and resistance were never strong, decided that he could not face another year of trying to teach English literature to the indifferent, in what was to him an inhospitable climate. Already, some months before, he had taken a leave of absence and gone in early winter to Bisbee, near the Arizona-Mexico border, where my mother and I, traveling in the berths of the Santa Fe, crowded with soldiers, later joined him. (I did not go to school at all that winter.) This change of scene had not been sufficient. Taking another leave and renting the house, he packed us into the car and started for Texas. His maladjustment sprang certainly from concrete difficulties but reflected also a vein of Irish melancholy that offset his solid practical sense. He did not drink, however: a good thing, as he said, for I think he could not have endured both liquor and life. These moves and later ones were doubtless very hard on my mother, who did not share his need for changing scenes and sloughing off the old self. She did have the generosity to agree to this move—whether without complaint, I cannot say. (She may have been sensitive to the unfortunate example set by her friend Estie, a maniac about housekeeping and an utter tyrant over her husband; the first result of her tyranny was that he was not allowed to sit in his own living room; the second was that their son, not having any model of real manhood, acquired the tastes of a woman.) Four years later, my father having quit his job in October in a fit of ire, Mother participated in a more radical uprooting, in which the house and furniture were sold and the family set off again like gypsies for the Big Bend country. On a much later occasion, when Father wanted to move permanently to England and live off of expedients and his small investments, she refused. He died soon after (his last words were "I'm restless"), and she had ample time to reflect on her decision. I do not blame her, however; my sins have been worse.

We left in a green Chevrolet sedan with running boards. It was Mother who had taught my father to drive in her boxy red coupé, but it had been replaced by a larger model, suitable for a family—at least a family of three. Whether the third—I—was supposed to have been born I wonder. Depression marriages produced few children; almost all of my school friends had no siblings or one at most, and, as my husband says about himself, they may have been strained through a dime-store diaphragm. Moreover, my parents' marriage was an odd one, and they might have preferred to remain a twosome. True, when they were married, in 1933, they were not so badly off as many; they both had jobs in the Denver schools, though as soon as the school board found out about the marriage, one of them had to quit. (Lord, it should have been my father. Mother could have kept us going better than he did, with less strain. But mores did not allow such; he would have been dishonored in his parents' eyes.) The important fact was that my mother was much older than my father—so much so that not only was her age never stated at home, the subject was never broached; and I grew up thinking that the age of parents was something never talked about, improper—like pregnancy and so forth. (Fortunately for her, the destruction by fire of all the records in the Colorado Springs courthouse, around 1900, allowed her to claim any birth date before then.) In 1933 Father was a youngish man, barely launched on his first profession, one that had brought them together. He had done student teaching in her classroom, and was paid very badly. She was well past the prime age for childbearing.

This age difference they handled very well, I now believe; but it may have been socially difficult, especially since Mother's hair had turned prematurely gray. Gide, who married his cousin, some two years older, reports hearing someone speak of her as "your mother." Only once was that mistake made in my presence concerning my parents. But speculation concerning ages and even parlor psychoanalysis must have abounded. Who doesn't know that every man wants to marry his mother, like Oedipus? Or perhaps, as illustrated, for instance, in Sartre's incestuous reveries, his sister—and Mother was exactly the age of my father's elder sister. (And, since we are on the topic, who dares to doubt that every woman wants to marry her father—which doubtless explains, to the credulous, why I, the daughter of a man named Paul, married another Paul, and my husband, the son of a Katherine, married me.) *They* handled it well, I said; but perhaps I did not. Or was it simply a difference of temperament that separated my mother and me, not a difference of age such that she could have been my grandmother? I really should have been a boy; she, poor thing, wanted a real girl. I had no use for dolls; all that interested me was climbing trees, batting at "work-up" in the street, playing explorer, and other male activities. (They led to two broken arms and two serious burns, one that came from falling from a rooftop into an ashpit—all worrisome and expensive, of course.)

Leaving Denver, we drove to Manitou Springs and then over Ute Pass to Woodland Park, where my uncle Ray was head of that section of the Pike National Forest. Ute Pass is not one of the highest passes through the Front Range; but the road was narrow then, with abundant curves and steep inclines. Like every other mountain trip we took, this was the occasion for much lamentation from my mother. Born in Colorado Springs, she nevertheless did not like to be in the mountains—better to look at them than to go up in them, she thought—and liked even less the unguarded precipices and sharp curves of mountain roads. Moreover, she had been in an accident in which the red coupé had turned over. There were whimperings and complaints and even a few tears, for which I had no patience at all. Only later did I come to realize that it was my father who was the true *grand nerveux,* to use Proust's term; Mother's nervousness was merely superficial.

The ranger station was on a rise some miles from town, with a broad and unimpeded view of Pike's Peak. The house combined some modern amenities with features of a mountain cabin. Behind the residence and office were a barn and an earthen cellar—cool

and private retreats. Since the electric lighting was not always reliable, each room had a tall kerosene lamp. Telephone service was
similarly primitive: one spoke loudly into the mouthpiece of a
wooden box affixed to the wall and hoped for a connection. The
cooking was done on a massive iron stove, with a large well for
heating water and a griddle for Uncle Ray's flapjacks. My uncle
was a master *raconteur* in his quiet Western way, and entertained us
with stories about the stolen bridge he had recovered (someone
had actually hauled it upstream) and about a night he had spent in
New Mexico, in a hovel so filthy that he dared not lie down: instead, he had kept himself and his hosts up until dawn by telling
stories.

Once down from the higher altitudes we were in the baking
heat of southern Colorado—Walsenburg, Trinidad—in a landscape whose barrenness was relieved by the Culebras and Sangre
de Cristo ranges to the west. We crossed Raton Pass in New Mexico, then drove to Texline and Dalhart, at the top of the Panhandle.
This is where Larry McMurtry ended the trek he describes in his
superb *In a Narrow Grave,* a trek like ours, except that Larry made
it in the opposite direction and expressly for the pleasure of seeing
his home state as a whole: a sort of meditation-in-motion by
which he hoped to totalize his understanding. We progressed
down the immense plains and their little towns, scattered like islands; we stopped early and stayed in small tourist courts, adorned
if not shaded by a few scrawny trees. The cottages, always clean,
smelled of pinewood and Lux or Cashmere Bouquet soap, and
often had tiny kitchens and alcoves where I would sleep. (The later
development of national motel chains, with mostly plastic inte-
riors and no surprises, does not constitute unqualified progress,
and I have been pleased to note that in West Texas most of the
towns are still too insignificant to attract Ramada and Holiday
Inns.) With the evening breeze coming off the Llano Estacado, and
the slight shade of a few shrubs, the cabins seemed cool, certainly by comparison to the daytime heat, which made a bottle of
Dr Pepper expode on me one afternoon. This was the region of
the Comanches and the huge cattle drives; I sang to myself cow-
boy songs about the railroad corral and troubles on the Old Chis-

holm Trail. With unlimited views of plain and sky, one could imagine oneself as close to the land as those who had wrung from it a difficult livelihood.

This too represents a mythology, but one not necessarily to be rejected. It is not a question for us now of misreading the past to make it what it was not—a bucolic idyll—but of seeing that we were formed by the vision of a man on his land, morally and politically free, and that if we are wholly separated from it we will lose not only a common memory but a dimension of our psyche and the grounding for some of our civic institutions. It is partly because of this shared sense of place and emphasis on the land that it has been possible for me to write like a southerner, although in my bones I belong to the West. This pastoral vision is probably still congenial to human beings generally—we started out, after all, as hunters and gatherers, and most of our forebears then lived off the fields, up until the middle of this century. Soviet psychologists have shown that industrial workers perform much more efficiently and keep in better spirits if their workshops are painted with outdoor scenes—the vaster the better (rolling plains, the ocean). We are told that we benefit, physically and mentally, from getting outdoors, going hunting, fishing, or hiking; when he felt well enough, my father was a great one for trout fishing. Even the supposed ranch-style houses of suburbs, with their insipid bluegrass lawns—which bear little resemblance to ranches I have known and make me glad that, since I am tied to an urban life, at least I live among houses designed for a nineteenth-century city—express doubtless a deep impulse to work the land and be master of all one surveys. I note even that a mail-order company is now selling wooden cutout cows, life-size, for decorating urban spreads.

I do not delude myself into thinking that ranching in the early days and riding the Chisholm Trail can have had much in common with the modern American's ersatz outdoor experience; it was hard, dirty, ill-paid, sometimes dangerous work, and, most of all, it was usually imposed by circumstances rather than chosen. But the fact that some did it, if only to grub out a few dollars, and thereby said no to other ways of surviving, means something. A

French social historian writing in 1975 argued that his nation had changed more in the previous twenty years than in the seventy-five years between the Franco-Prussian War and the close of World War II. Similarly radical changes have marked the United States in the past three or four decades, particularly in urbanization; even if what I saw in 1944 was no longer marked by the cattle drives of the nineteenth century, it *was* a world in which one could still make a living, if not a good one, on a small ranch, and in which men did what their fathers and grandfathers had done before them, rather than going to Dallas to work in a brokerage firm. As a way of reconciling this new economy with older values, the cut-out cows are not satisfactory. Sending fifty million people at a time to refresh themselves in the national parks and forests is not a practical or appealing solution either; nor, despite their apparent utility, would Soviet-style murals suffice. Still less acceptable is the view that the old frontier values can be maintained or revived by the unlimited ownership of firearms. One would like to think that the written word, and especially the pastoral tradition, could be instrumental in calling attention, at least, to what the land offered, but since its effectiveness has been proven tragically limited, to hope for much from poetry would be delusion.

South of San Antonio, my parents began looking for a place to spend a year. In most of the far-flung towns, little had been built for years, I believe, and they had none of the slick roadside commercialism that is the mark nowadays of prosperity. I remember in particular Alice. The tourist court was shaded by fine pecan trees, under which we ate some peaches after supper; my mother, usually so careful, left her good paring knife there, a loss she bemoaned for years. Now I bemoan hers. There and in Kingsville, she inquired about the possibilities of teaching for a year. Nothing was available until we hit the extreme Lower Rio Grande Valley, where she found a job as a history teacher in Edinburg and my father, after some weeks, signed on as "circulation manager" for the daily newspaper.

When he was younger he had taken some vocational test, which had indicated he would be outstanding as an insurance salesman. Perhaps, given his warm, outgoing manner, that would have been so, except for one thing: he was quite incapable of urging people to spend their money for what they could ill afford, and a hard sell was as foreign to him as thievery. But a part-time job peddling subscriptions to a small paper was a different story. In the green Chevrolet he covered all the towns along the river, following the narrow roads through the citrus groves. He liked the work; his employers must not have been very demanding about results. Sometimes he would take me with him, through the groves, where workers would give us grapefruit the size of canteloupe and oranges almost as large. To this day I avoid if possible all California citrus fruit, not only because I dislike California in general, with its evils as various as malls, beachboys, skateboards, and sour cream on Mexican food, but because the Texas fruit is far superior to the tasteless Sunkist products, with their artificial color and thick skins.

Housing in the valley was inadequate for the population, swollen because of Harlingen Air Base. We found something in a quadruplex owned by the Valerys. They were from Alabama; I suppose they had sold land there earlier and moved to the valley for their retirement, where they made do with a little rental income. I remember her as a moist, big-bosomed woman who, even to her husband's face, called him "Mr. Valery." His favorite expression probably condensed his life's experience: "You can't get all the possums up one tree." At the end of our stay, he wrote in my autograph book: "The touchstone of progress and key to success / Can always be found in doing your best"—a practical and moral precept with which I dare not disagree entirely, but whose imperfect rhyme bothered me. We lived downstairs, next to them. Upstairs was a Mrs. Fox—perhaps a widow—with her daughter Betty, my age. Next to them was the Frost family. The father must have been in the military service. Mrs. Frost worked. She sometimes appeared on the steps clad only in a bra and shorts. Her housekeeping standards were abysmal: roaches and palmetto bugs bred and gamboled unmolested. Fred and Sara Beth, who were in adolescence, fended for themselves much of the time. One day Fred ate what he thought was some soup in a pot on the stove; it turned out to be the lukewarm dishwater that no one had thrown out.

Each of the apartments consisted of three rooms in a row, plus a back porch. I slept in the living room. All winter long no cover heavier than a cotton blanket was necessary. The reader can reflect on the implications of this concerning the hot months, in a town as yet without air conditioning. We used cheap Fireking glass dishes from the dimestore—the sort that collectors now buy at garage sales and antique shows. The water was so foul that even strong coffee, which my mother had taken to drinking to offset the effects of the steamy, soporific afternoons, could not conceal its taste.

South Texas, as I remember it then, combined features of the more western parts of the state with a humid climate and heavy rainfall. Land that was still used for grazing purposes looked god-awful—nothing but chaparral, mostly mesquite and huisache, covered with thorns (hence the necessity of chaps). But the citrus groves were luxuriant, the trees almost as sculpted and symmetrical as in topiary, the leaves dark and waxy. And in nearby McAllen, splendid royal palms lined the avenue, and bougainvillea and hibiscus spilled over the patio walls. Around our quadruplex, the vegetation was more like that of the chaparral: athel trees (an unappealing relative of the Mediterranean tamarisk), huisache, and prickly pear. Instead of growing close to the ground in clumps, as it does farther west, the pear rose ten feet or more in height—a grotesque piling up of drab cubist planes bearing spiny and discolored fruit.

A number of small happenings of the year remain vivid, as if standing for the rest. When it rained over eleven inches one afternoon the water had nowhere to go except up. Everyone at school, from the principal on down, rolled up trousers and took off shoes and trod home in currents and eddies that were certainly very dirty and probably snake-infested. We watched the wavelets lapping at the steps and the first boards of the back porch: not without reason had the house been raised a foot or so on blocks. That evening frogs by the hundreds sang from their newly formed marshes, in concert with the mockingbirds. I have since learned to expect this almost every year in New Orleans, but to someone from the arid West it was like the biblical deluge. Another memory is of visiting

Reynosa and Matamoros in Mexico, despite my father's microphobia. It was in Edinburg that I began learning Spanish, and although I have spent much of my adult life reading and reflecting on French literature, Spanish remains a first love, forever connected in my mind with border towns, tacky though they be, their shops filled with pottery, baskets, and silver, their cantinas dispensing into the streets mournful Mexican love ballads. In the spring we visited Padre Island, now a resort with high-rise hotels but then almost pristine. At a Brownsville hotel during that excursion, a waiter greeted us at breakfast time with a curt announcement that cut off any hopeful inquiry: "No ham, no bacon, no sausage." Another peculiarity was learning in school to sing the Soviet national anthem. I do not misremember: Allied unity was taken seriously.

Two deaths marked the year for us. One was Roosevelt's, in April. I had been born under his administration and there had so far been more monarchs on the throne of England during my lifetime than American presidents. My father disliked the man, but he had taken me to see him in Denver two or three years before; the president had passed in an open car just a few feet from my grandparents' front porch on Alameda Avenue. The other death was that of my uncle Jack, who died of burns, in the lifeboat, after his destroyer was attacked in the Battle of Leyte Gulf. The event represented the eruption of violent history into our lives and brought us into a community of millions. Perhaps my father, who had been exceptionally close to him, never recovered fully; his melancholy certainly did not improve, and his dislike of war, which led him once into conversing with a Jehovah's Witness with whom he had little in common but that, seemed to color much of his thinking thenceforth. In June he decided to return to Colorado, perhaps with the conviction that he must try once again to wrestle with a normal life—or was it simply that he had decided the climate of the valley was malarial and worse than the cold? The return trip seemed even longer, but we had the pleasure of seeing again Kingsville, Fredericksburg, Brownfield, and the other towns that had charmed us on the way down, and, one day when we were lucky, eating a good chicken-fried steak in a Panhandle café. I was still a child, and the war was over in Europe; but Nagasaki and Hiroshima were about to bring to the world a new sense of terror and conclude forever a long period of history called the pre-atomic age.

Prospecting

The summer I was fifteen, at a Girl Scout camp in Colorado called the Flying-G Ranch, I was one of a number of experienced campers who had worked themselves up through the ranks to the privileged class called Prospectors. It had taken me five summers to reach that rank, and since the following autumn my family left Colorado for good to settle in the Big Bend of Texas, it was my last stay at the Flying-G. It was also my last summer of close camaraderie with girls only. Tonight, when over forty years separate me from what I was then, I am going prospecting again, digging down through the layers, sifting through the running stream of memory. Those who have never been fifteen will probably not read the account that follows; let others think back to their own summer of content, when they could feel and live themselves fully among those of their sex, before that easy companionship was altered by the need for another.

With the word *prospecting,* images come to mind of lore I read as a girl concerning the silver and gold rushes, and the loners who made their way through the tortuous valleys and up the steep slopes and ravines with small packs—usually on a donkey—and what they thought was a keen eye, usually sharpened by desperation. On a larger scale, I think of the old mining towns my family used to drive through, such as Silver Plume and Georgetown, on the way to Loveland Pass—towns mostly run down but where some mining operations were still functioning—and of the evidence of frenzy, failure, and great fortunes—the opera house and saloons of Central City, the Leadville opera house and the theater that Horace Tabor built for Baby Doe in Denver with some of the thousands from the Little Pittsburgh Mine.

The mining analogy is not perfect for my undertaking, however; for no matter how unburdened they were with worldly goods, even the poorest of those who went prospecting in the

Colorado mountains had at least a pick and shovel or a flat metal
pan—tools that extend man's instrumentality in the world beyond
his body. And they were looking for something external to themselves. I, on the contrary, am searching within myself, and it is
that same self that must do the searching. This epistemological
problem by which the means and the end are the same is paralleled
in all attempts to discern the truth of the exterior world, since
reason—the chief tool of investigation—is unable ultimately to
ratify itself. This old dilemma, identified by the Greeks in a form
called the paradox of the Cretan liar, might seem sufficient to
make one throw out reason in despair—except that throwing out
the mind is not really possible, barring self-induced insanity, and
even that is a form of mind.

Happily, to offset this limitation in the mind's ability to investigate itself, there is a complementary strength, in the fact that
mind always takes a perspective on itself, by a self-reflexive process that passes through knowledge of the world and self-in-the-
world and goes on constantly, ranging from the most primitive
self-awareness to the elaborate creations of consciousness in the
form of philosophy and art. Moreover—to return to my metaphor—unlike the chaps who took up prospecting in the Colorado
mountains and elsewhere and who were usually poor both before
and after (Tabor was an exception in the latter respect, until he
went bankrupt in 1893 and died penniless), I am already rich in the
treasures of remembrance and reflection and know that other dis-
coveries can add to this wealth. Furthermore, I am really not entirely without tools, at least if language, despite its limitations,
illustrated, again, in the Cretan liar paradox, can be considered
something that, born of the mind, nevertheless can go beyond
what *was* and *is* to discover or create something new, transcend-
ing its material. Finally, according to its etymology, *to prospect*
means to look ahead, and so, going over territory of the past, I
am, like a miner imagining what he will do with his find, really
looking forward to the uses to which its disclosures can be put.

My first visit to the Flying-G had been, as I said, some years
before, in the summer of 1945, when my parents returned to
Colorado after the year spent in the Lower Rio Grande Valley of

Texas barely in time to get me enrolled—for a week only, given finances. The camp was located in the Pike National Forest near Bailey, southwest of Denver, not far from my grandmother's cabin, toward Kenosha Pass. Part of it had been a working ranch at one time, and in one of the back areas there was an abandoned sawmill. We rode up in old busses. I liked it immediately, despite such features as cold nights, outdoor showers with creek water, and the rule requiring that all plates had to be entirely empty at the end of the meal, which meant that I had to consume liver. (Rather than leading me to acquire an eclectic taste, the regimen at the Flying-G just made me wary. At cocktail parties, before biting into any canapé, I always ask the server or hostess whether it contains chicken or goose liver. The practice is not the height of social nicety. But once, at least, I found a sympathetic hostess who assured me she wouldn't offer me anything so undesirable.)

Campers were grouped by age; the different classes ate together and sometimes shared activities but lived in separate units, whose distance—up to a mile or so—from the main lodge was a token of their seniority. We slept on cots in large tents—army surplus, doubtless—and had primitive latrines. What was done for washing of clothes and person (apart from the infrequent cold showers) I really don't remember—probably precious little. But *some* laundry was done. One later summer when I was there longer, I had two identical cast-off polo shirts from twins who lived near us. Switching them, I wore one while the other was in the dirty-clothes bag or drying (to the degree that was possible, because although Colorado is in an arid zone, rain falls in the mountains nearly every afternoon in summer). Later I learned that a fellow camper had complained to her mother that Catharine never changed her shirt.

Activities were of five or six sorts: softball but no other team sport; crafts, which I cared little for and succeeded at accordingly; hiking, by far my favorite; music; horseback riding; and lessons in outdoorsmanship. Some equestrian skills I must have acquired, for not many summers ago across the river from New Orleans, I managed to feel comfortable on the back of an old nag; but it was never my joy to find myself cantering down a steep trail on a horse who was taking me for a ride instead of my taking him—or, more pointedly, to be thrown off and roll down among the underbrush. The music was primitive, in a sense: no instruments at all, if memory serves me. But that helped us acquire good pitch, and I learned dozens of songs, many of which still pop into my vocal chords when, free again in a sense, I am driving over the open ranges or mountains of West Texas or New Mexico. We may have done some study of the area; in those days I was interested in geology and botany, and now vaguely remember adding a bit to my knowledge there. On Sundays there were Christian services led by counselors under the pines—the sort of worship in God's own temple that would have appealed to the Romantic poets. (The Catholic girls were bussed into town, however.) Then there were chores—quite numerous and to be taken seriously, since the staff was small and there was no pretense of coddling us. Anyway, we were not sissies, and to this day I find it difficult to tolerate a sissy of either sex.

All of this does not sound like much; but it was a compatible routine, I liked the counselors and most of my fellow-campers, and we were in splendid mountain territory, marked by meadows and streams at the low points, forested slopes with pine and Douglas fir beginning just above the glades, and the high crests rising farther on. In some ways the setting must have been crucial to the pleasure, if I judge by the fact that later experiences at camps—a church establishment in southern New Mexico, a camp for college girls in Michigan, a Scout camp at Mitre Peak in the Big Bend where I was a counselor one summer—seemed incomplete, inauthentic; but perhaps it was a question of age, not altitude and topography.

In any case, the camp routine itself was so congenial to me that nostalgia for it remains. If, in my thirties, I doubtless enjoyed more than anyone else a few days' work reading Advanced Placement exams in French at the Educational Testing Service in New Jersey, it was because, living on a campus in dormitories, rising with the sun and eating in chow lines, and working on a collective task in a spirit of good fellowship, the team recreated for me something of the Flying-G spirit. Does this inclination explain why, over and above my general taste for both Romanesque and Gothic architecture, I am particularly attracted to monasteries of those styles, where the sense of communal life is visible in the very design—enclosed garden, central fountain, communal walkways, and chapel all bespeaking the same shared enterprise?

The effects may be deeper still. There is something in me that calls for communal enterprises—perhaps less *living* in common, which can be appealing but is, strictly speaking, chiefly just a maintaining of life—than common projects and goals, as though the best of human effort—that which goes to remake the world (in any sense you wish to give to the term except the artistic one)—should, by its nature, be a shared undertaking. Those who direct institutions and agencies these days—as well as coaches, from whom they took the metaphor—would call my attitude that of a "team player." Well, yes, and it shows itself, I suppose, in the fact that, poet and maverick though I am, I work well with others in the small world of a family, a group of friends, a department of French and Italian . . . Because of my belief in the common enterprise, egalitarianism in such contexts is my rule, and I am pleased to say that in the aforesaid French department we have at once maintained faculty morale and dealt more effectively with students by having all professors teach at all levels rather than cordoning off the young assistant professors in quarantine with the freshmen. (When I differ with the others on a matter of principle, however, no amount of appeal to team interests is effective as far as I am concerned. The spirit of expediency has too many adherents already.)

But I have in mind goals that go beyond the quotidian ones of these collectivities, something political and social on a wide scale, something visionary. (Nothing like a pragmatist who wants to go beyond pragmatism. Worse, however, is a determinist who leaps over his own determinism into idealism.) The only problem is that socialism simply does not work, and especially not when it is applied in the large-scale enterprises that constitute a nation's principal means of production; surely in our century we should have learned that, if little else. (Academic Marxists are, to be sure, an exception.) The communes of the late 1960s and 1970s—of which

I was never a part, it must be specified—broke up in a matter of years, showing that even the small-scale society in which Rousseau envisioned citizens living according to the general will is too fragile for practicality. It took longer of course for the socialist behemoth of the Soviet Union to crack, a time proportional to the depth and breadth of its tyranny. The socialists of the nineteenth century who founded (partly on a model by Charles Fourier) such centers as Brook Farm, the Oneida Community of New York, and New Harmony, Indiana, and who were, I wager, generally more principled and more humane than their twentieth-century Communist successors, were similarly unable to make their vision endure, even in the New World, then a wilderness. Why this should be so I will leave to others to continue investigating, saying only that, to judge by the implications of Rousseau's notion of the general will and by what major revolutions have shown, there is no tyranny like that of the collectivity, which, notwithstanding the idea that it is composed of the will of all, always ends up represented by a director—Rousseau's Legislator—or oligarchy—one that then uses the position to advance its self-interest.

The Prospectors at the Flying-G were the elite, occupying the farthest site—and a beautiful one—and having less stringent regulations than the younger girls. We had an outstanding leader, too. The counselors bore nicknames—"Robin," "Ranger," and so on; but this one went by her genuine nickname, Ginger. She was the young wife of a U.S. Forest Service ranger in the Carson National Forest of New Mexico. I suppose that the income from this work—meager though it must have been—was a significant supplement to the similarly meager salary of her husband. During my visits to that state in recent years, I have wondered whether she was still settled there, in the wilderness to which she was so attached and for which she proved, to us, such an able and challenging guide. For she, with another, took us on a pack trip of several days into the higher country—the exclusive privilege of the Prospectors. Donkeys were loaded with the sleeping bags and chow supplies; we carried our other gear on our backs. Mine included an old canteen that one of my uncles had used in the army during World War I. I wonder whether Ginger carried a firearm of

19

any sort. Nowadays, one might be apprehensive concerning who might be found in the mountains—or who might find us. Even then, there must have been strange mountain men around—as there had been since the previous century—some just eccentric, others dangerous.

Even if I lived in that area again, I could not begin now to trace our route. We used back roads some of the time, trails the rest. In that latitude, in the summer, the sun rises very early. Waking shortly after four, I think, we made breakfast over a fire (outdoor cooking skills had been part of our lessons in earlier years), packed the donkeys, doused the coals, then started out on the trail. I had a pair of ill-fitting boots and a leather jacket bought at a men's store; the boots, I remember, stiffened even more after we waded through a creek or so. Blisters and fatigue were part of a day's trek; another annoyance was the fact that we were not allowed to drink from streams, since there were cattle in some of the valleys. (I suppose that, given the date, this interdiction reflected genuine concern for our well-being, not just the fear that the Scout Council of Colorado would be sued if someone picked up dysentery.) We ate a cold lunch by the side of the trail, then hiked on a few more miles before staking out a camp for the evening.

A main chore was preparing the fire, which was to serve two purposes—cooking and campfire for after-dinner fellowship. (Although the evenings were very chilly—I slept in an Army surplus goosedown mummy bag—the fire would not have been expected to furnish much warmth; as those who have been camping know, smoke and possibly being singed are what one usually gets if one approaches close enough to feel the heat.) We had campfires back at the lodge, also, but they usually included all the campers; this one was our own, intimate, serving purposes both practical and spiritual. As the food tasted even better at that altitude, after a day of hiking and chores, so the songs sounded clearer in the thin, cold air, and the flame of fellowship burned more brightly.

Sensitive as we are today to sexual questions, one is obliged to ask whether, in this fellowship, which had an odor of what the French call a *gynécée* (a residence for women, or harem), there was

20

a Sapphic suggestion. One need only glance at the newspaper or watch the nightly news from time to time to see that, when from institutions, even family and school, is peeled away what turns out to be only the veneer of propriety that used to cover them and which, it was erroneously thought, constituted their inner reality also, all sorts of unsavory things come to light. Pedophiles have cloaked themselves in the garments of celibate priest or Boy Scout leader. (A recent and notorious case in New Orleans involved a priest who was also a professor of history in my very institution—indeed housed across the hall from me—who picked up waifs in the French Quarter and took them home to the rectory, where he filmed them in forbidden activities, quite under the nose of fellow priests; after exposure, he went to a college on Staten Island. It turns out that he also left the priesthood, married, had a child, and has returned recently to the Crescent City.) What about those who are attracted to gatherings of adolescent girls? Of course I cannot speak for everyone in the group with which I associated that summer. But, as far as I can discern, there was nothing equivocal on anyone's part; certainly for me it was friendship only. We were fifteen and sixteen; we had learned to be friends on the basis of our common sex, without its being an interference.

This sort of fellowship with women is rare and getting rarer. Recently I attended a luncheon given by a Tulane official for the women faculty. Alas, the gathering, which I had hoped to enjoy, turned more or less into a rally against men; some faculty members actually stood up to report, in a sneering manner, that their research in such-and-such area of social science had proven how superior women were to their rivals, and others stridently reported plans for wresting from them still more power. It is a sad day when a woman feels uncomfortable at a gathering of her own.

The end of the pack trip broke the intensity with which we had lived and hiked together, and then, some days later, the conclusion of camp brought to an end the general communal life shared there. It was not the conclusion of the summer; there remained tennis and biking in Denver, and seeing a close friend, confined to bed, with whom I had gone to summer school at East High earlier that summer to take advanced Spanish from my father's friend Arnold

Ward. But these experiences were aleatory, contingent; those with the Prospectors had something essential about them. School started a little later, and I spent a few weeks in classes in Denver before my father decided to go to Texas again. The Scout friends I had had (some for years) were replaced gradually by new acquaintances—more or less the entire high school in the small town where we settled; and the sort of teenage life that was the only one available to us—movies, hamburgers at the drive-in, a few parties, the class proms—took the place of the camp routine and its fellowship. The whole was a quick moment.

Why should I bother to write about this? Just because that summer was marked by happiness is not a reason—although it is true that there are some adults who are so bereft of satisfactory memories from their childhood or adolescence that they find nearly incomprehensible the desire to return, if only in words, to that past, and thus my good fortune is noteworthy; reflecting on that, I am not without gratitude to parents who made possible for me so many good weeks at the Flying-G. Lest it be thought, however, that I knew nothing but a serene contentment at *any* time of my life, I shall note that, despite vitality and eagerness for activity, I suffered as a child a great deal of anguish, maybe of a metaphysical sort, if you consider the question of the meeting of world and will to be a metaphysical one. Then there were the problems of beginnings, matter—*why* matter?—and nothingness. When my own daughter was younger, I saw some of the same in her, but perhaps, rather than being a matter of our particular heredity, angst is simply common to the human condition. In any case, being strong-willed and antisocial in a world formed around social units, where conformity is expected, especially of the young as they are being shaped, made for some very difficult moments, for me and, doubtless, my poor parents; *I* did not care, certainly, what the girl at camp thought of my polo shirt but my mother was probably chagrined at the remark.

That is why camp was so well suited for me, or me for it; for such concerns about dress were not the rule: patched jeans were quite acceptable and the adolescent craze for makeup, fancy hairstyles, and so on was not so prevalent then and had not penetrated much the Flying-G. Furthermore—and this is important—the routine and customs were rational in terms of the aims of the camp, which I had chosen and accepted freely, whereas dozens of social usages in my ordinary world had absolutely no rationality for me at the time—for example, the requirement that a dress be worn, or the pressing need for me to accompany my mother on a charitable visit to an old woman she knew, who lived in a dingy walk-up and smelled strongly of a licorice-based patent medicine and urine. I suppose that, as a whole, many of my efforts as an adult have been spent in trying to make my life a *rational* one—whereby its uses and its aims would correspond. Only then does it make sense to me and do the corresponding customs really find favor. On the other hand, I recognize the need for manners; indeed they make life possible. But that means they are rational, even if arbitrary. So I have merely broadened, not rejected, my adolescent understanding of what makes sense.

The question still remains to be answered: what is the use of remembering? Perhaps that is another way of asking what the uses of the past may be. Historians tell us, do they not, that those who do not remember the past are condemned to repeat it. They do not take their own enterprise, surely, in only that negative way—the investigation of something to be avoided—nor would anyone propose seriously that memory is to serve only that purpose. Much of what has happened *is* to be avoided, of course, and if research and study at any level will help prevent future atrocities and injustices and alleviate what would otherwise be misery, why the libraries of historical studies and the millions of hours invested, collectively, by often unwilling students are certainly worthwhile. Yet a great deal of formal history is cultural history, in a positive sense: the investigation, for instance, through archeological and textual research, of what the houses of the prosperous were like in Egypt around 1500 B.C., or of the founding of the basilica in Vézelay and the struggles of various factions over it; the study of the development of poetry and religious cults; the recreation of life in a medieval village. And we assume that, in some way, this is connected to ourselves, no matter how remotely. Can one speak of something analogous in the individual, a cultural self, connected to the present, to investigate which memory serves as a sort of archeological tool? But a human being is not a cultural artifact.

Perhaps one should take up the psychoanalytic model instead and suppose that, in the investigation of one's childhood or adolescence, repressed experiences will be revealed that will explain, and help resolve, the neuroses of the present. That would be, it can be argued, of very great use indeed. It would, though, require an analyst to draw from the analysand these secrets, and the unconscious would be valorized at the expense of the rational faculty. Such are not my ways and I suspect that a good deal of what passes for psychoanalytic remembrance, or at least the conclusions drawn from it, is bogus. In any case, like Gide, who believed that the Freudian analysis a specialist proposed to do on him would destroy the fount of his art, I like my neuroses, if so they be. Perhaps I can even claim, like one of my students, a delightful poet, referring to the year she was fourteen, "I was neurotic before my time."

Then there is the model of Proust who, no doubt about it, drew from cultivated remembrance—incorporating however into the powerful affective element an enormous quantity of observations and reflections on society, nature, art and literature, love, travel, friendship, human character, and other topics—a monumental opus, a sort of encyclopedia of experience. But, in the first place, it would be absurd for me, or any writer that has recently come to my attention, to pretend to rival Proust. One would risk ridicule. In the second place, merely to contemplate the past narcissistically, recounting childhood traumas or, as an early and hostile reader of Proust put it, describing how one used to turn over in bed, without drawing from the memory process something exterior to the self, is tedious at best and probably unhealthy. Finally, there is such a thing as the future also, with which I am not unconcerned. One way, then, of looking at this question of girlhood experience and its recall is to ask what relationship it bears to the present and future; as Anatole France wrote, "The future is made only with the past." In other terms, did camping prepare us (as the Girl

Scout officials sometimes claim) for life? Can the experience have meaning in the present and future?

Now, a person is never fully prepared for life except by living it; it is in the midst of experience, or perhaps only after, that the synthetic relationship between needs and means, preparation and fulfillment, becomes clear. Retrospectively, one sees connections, favorable or unfavorable, between one act and another, one state of mind and another; but the "preparation" is itself life, and what follows is always prelude to something still further. I am not, to be sure, speaking of the practical plane, or what might be called the *techniques* of living (acquiring a basic education, vocational skills and so on, a way with people, or just plain horse sense). In the sense of techniques, few things learned at the Flying-G have proven useful, though recently I have had some occasion to build fires and cook outdoors; perhaps, in addition, the enforced cooperation with others served me well, and the outdoor life was good for helping me acquire strength and endurance (as Valéry said about Sisyphus, "He develops his muscles"). Certainly the experience, along with others, contributed to my sense of our stewardship of nature.

Essentially, however, camp did not prepare me for life; it *was* life. To inquire about its meaning is like asking the purpose of life. Auden, I believe, is the one who remarked in that connection, "We are here to help others. We do not know what others are here for." A number of philosophers have treated the matter with less brevity. To return to the historical analogy, I said that the human being is not a cultural *artifact*—because we are not fixed; but, like history as a whole, we are cultural insofar as we are both process and product of culture. Indeed, we speak of *cultivating* potentiality. What is the good of such cultivation in the long run? Well, in the long run, as Keynes said, we'll all be dead. My view is that the meaning of the camp was in the camping, for itself; even if it bore no connection to my present, it would still be valid, and the process of memory would be all the more justified as a recreation of something otherwise unavailable that had been one with the person. What memory means, in fact, is significance in the present.

Both process and product count. Perhaps my awareness of this explains why, except for a few periods, such as a year of study in France and some other moving moments, I have not kept a journal. A diary from the Flying-G years would, it is true, furnish now many curious facts; but it would be dead letter without the spirit that was both identical to it and went beyond it. Nor do I carry around a camera—not only because I do not want that protuberance hanging at the level of my navel. What I have forgotten cannot be essential, for as the self bends over the past it identifies what it responds to, vibrates with—what it recognizes; the rest is worth little. That is what memory teaches us—the discovery of the essential. It is the sifting and shaping of experiences through time that resonates through Proust's work and through anyone's process of recall; what is put down on paper or saved like photographs is, as he indicated himself, of little value until consciousness recreates from its own depths the novel of the self.

Desert Silvery Blue

It is near midnight, on a cold Texas evening in spring, and we are riding in Mrs. Blucher's car along U.S. highway 90 (in its vintage version), coming back from San Antonio. The stars so saturate the sky that they seem ready to precipitate out. Like a rough skin, the desert stretches everywhere over the hills and ridges and the crumpled folds in between, until it cracks at the horizon. Clumps of cactus and modest desert verbena shape the roadside, and occasionally, a sentinel lechuguilla stands stark on the profile of a hill ahead. At moments there seems to be very little between my fifteen years and the deep, self-sufficient night.

> Desert silvery blue beneath the pale moonlight,
> Coyotes lapping lazy on the hill.
> Sleepy winks of light along the far skyline,
> Time for millin' cattle to be still.

This song of my earlier girlhood connects me to my own past—summers of camping out—and to the past and even the present of the cattle culture all around me.

Near Sanderson—still eighty-five miles from home—Mrs. Blucher, who has driven us to a state English competition, starts telling us about her own life—meeting her husband, an engineer, who came to work in the mercury mines at Terlingua near the Rio Grande; raising her children; the onset of what the poet Saint-John Perse calls the "grand age," which for her at the time must have been about fifty-five but to us makes her seem ancient. And in her words another life unfolds for me, one of the very few adult existences into which I have seen intimately, save those of family members, and even then . . . She speaks as if she supposes that we girls might ourselves eventually no longer be fifteen and sixteen, but be women, and married—that is, as though the adult feminine condition might in fact be ours sometime, as it has been hers. For more than an hour, she lives for us in words what it has taken her decades to live out in reality; we are entranced. At the same time, elsewhere in the same state, the man as yet unknown to me who will become my first husband is halfway through the university; farther away, a young Marine, Paul Brosman, will receive his M.A. in a few weeks, be commissioned, and leave for Quantico and then Korea. The enamel-bright stars too seem to shift, as if foreshadowing our necessary conjunctions and disjunctions.

Now, Olive Blucher, you are deceased, surely (my last visit to you, some while ago, was to a stooped little woman living in a trailer and looking like a mummy), and that age from which you shared your experience—paradoxically, as if speaking to equals— well, now I too have passed it, and I can write—I will have to—for both of us together, as well as several others who, for a time, put down roots among the greasewood and mesquite. "Home," to which we were returning, was Alpine, seat of Brewster County, "The Athens of West Texas," as my father facetiously called it, in the Big Bend, some 350 miles from San Antonio, 220 from El Paso, close to nothing . . . The curves in the old highway were abrupt, and the road was rising, ascending toward its high point, some 6,000 feet, just west of Alpine. Few cars were out; except for drivers going to California along the southernmost route, instead of the less mountainous U.S. 80, travelers were not common, and the ranchers were mostly home and in bed. Along some stretches the highway and the Southern Pacific lines parallel each other, and we passed a freight train or so, speeding along despite hauling probably more than a hundred cars. In later years I would come home from college twice a year by train over that route. It seems to me now that, of the moments of fear and love I have known, and even of joy—that brilliant claret of life—none has surpassed in keenness the anticipation I felt, trip after trip, hearing those final miles to home clatter away under the wheels, with the hills un- folding on both sides and the last glimmers of light hanging on at the horizon.

We reached Marathon, a town of some five hundred souls, al- most entirely dark by then; we had thirty-one miles to go. To the north, the Glass Mountains loomed in the darkness. "The mountains look on Marathon—and Marathon looks on the sea"—not, in this case, Byron's brilliant Aegean, but a sea of cactus, especially to the south, where U.S. highway 385, at that time the only paved road to Big Bend National Park, sinks into miles and miles of agave flats. My mother would later become devoted to Marathon, when, generous of herself as usual, she would drive every school day for the next five years to teach English there, partly so that she could pay for my college education at what was then known as the Rice Institute. In those days there was no tuition at Rice, and I even had a cash grant all four years and a modest job, but there were living and traveling expenses, plus books. My father was not at that time working at all—the 1950 census was his sole gainful employment—and Mother was working only as a part-time assistant for a professor in the English department at Sul Ross State College, but since that would not do permanently, the following year she signed on at Marathon. She had done a lot of teaching before—Torrington and Greybull, Wyoming; Edinburg, Texas; schools in Colorado—Denver, a country school at Fountain, and Colorado Military Academy with its bad boys; but she was no longer young, and this must have been a demanding job. There were no consolidated schools or school transportation in Brewster County. Ranchers who were well-to-do, or just comfortable, had houses in Alpine as well as on the ranch, or at least sent their children to board in town; the pupils at the Marathon school were the children of very modest families who worked for the railroad or ran a few small stores and services there, or they drove in from the surrounding ranches.

We had moved to Alpine the previous fall, when my father, in a fit of pique, quit his teaching job in Denver, sold the house, and packed us up, with a few things, to head south. Including the winter's leave he had spent in Arizona, and the full year's leave, during which we had gone to South Texas, this was the third time he had bidden good-bye to the Denver public schools, over which presided a Mr. Green, whom Father never tired of ridiculing and to whom he fantasized about sending boxes of roaches or dead snakes. Though he had done other things—for instance, a failed venture in the grocery business—teaching was what he was most born to, of all the types of labor by which man must earn his bread; generous-minded, well-read, and discerning, he taught literature with persuasiveness and sensitivity, and as a former student of his, now dean of a state university, told me, those who studied under him learned to do nothing less than their best. But Mr. Green and company had persisted in assigning him to the worst schools and the most unrewarding sorts of classes, and he had found himself in charge of courses in drivers' education and "human relations" (some primitive variety of sex education, I think). Moreover, as the last child of a tubercular mother who was simply worn out when he was born, he had never been strong, and Colorado winters, on top of his dissatisfaction and neurosis, were simply too awful to bear. So this time he had quit, in mid-October, for good.

He had picked out Alpine from the map, for reasons unknown to me. Well, it was dry and distant; and the college might have had something to do with it. Our first glimpse of the town had come as we arrived from Pecos, Balmorhea, and Fort Davis. This approach from the north brings one along Texas roads 17 and 118 through the Davis Mountains, the most forested of the whole area, with even a few running streams in the summer. Past the southernmost palisades of the range, Alpine lies ahead, lolling in a slight hollow, with Sul Ross Hill to the east, Twin Peaks and Paisano Peak to the west, low hills and Cathedral Mountain to the south, and range land—mostly the o6 Ranch—in between.

When we first reached town, we lived in married students' headquarters on the campus—basically a one-room cottage, intended for a young couple, not one with a teen-aged daughter. Shortly afterwards we moved to Mrs. Asa Jones's garage apartment, which at least had a separate living room, where I slept. My parents settled into the ways of a little town with ease. Father would go down to the post office twice a day to get the mail, which came by train—the Argonaut, with its old green cars, and the silvery Sunset Limited, the pride of the line. He would also stop by the Alpine Drug Store to buy a paper—often the San Antonio *Light*—just after they had been unloaded from the mail car right across the street. And he would pass the time of day with his friend Hefflin Bowden, who worked at the drug store and made money on the side by entering—and winning—contests of all descriptions. Sometimes after school Father met me for a Coke at the City Drug, which had a soda fountain. Mother graded papers at the college, joined the Methodist Church, made friends. I went to school, of course, worked on my music and Spanish, read, and, some months later, fell in love with a boy who, I am pleased to say at this remove, was worthy of it.

It was, to be sure, a very circumscribed life. For us students, this trip to San Antonio had been the major event of the school year, along with the band trip to El Paso for the Sun Bowl, complete with tequila in the back of the school bus—I did not partake—and a visit to Ciudad Juárez and its streets filled with barrooms. (My husband teases me to this day about "dancing at the Sun Bowl," but, really, I only played and marched, and we were clad in long pants—a good thing, since a cold wind was blowing through the Franklin Mountains.) Alpine was so small and so far from everywhere that, except to my father and a few old ranchers who knew better, cities—even a cowtown such as San Angelo—had an unhealthy appeal; many people burned up a lot of gasoline, and a few killed themselves, tearing back to town late at night, after a trip that was usually inconsequential, except for feminine purchases at the White House or Frost Bros. department store. With the exception of summer treks northward across New Mexico so that we could see family—"our people," as my aunt said—and spend some time in the Rockies, my father limited our excursions to drives closer by—Fort Davis, to eat at Indian Lodge, or, later, Marfa, to the west, where we had finally persuaded him to try the delectable Mexican food at Borunda's Café. Television had not arrived—cable hookups did not come until the 1970s— and many homes and ranches did not have phone service; in fact it was while he was installing phone lines near the Spur Ranch for the Big Bend Telephone Company years later that the son of friends of ours was electrocuted. There were, however, a paper, the *Avalanche,* and a radio station, KVLF, "The Voice of the Big Bend," with announcers whose spoonerisms, mispronunciations, malapropisms, and West Texas accent turned the 12:30 newscast—a ritual for us—into farce. ("The escapee was apprehended and reincarnated," for instance.) I must admit that we had music, too, in the form of dozens of good recordings, and plays, thanks to the college, where we saw Dan Blocker, later of "Bonanza," in *Othello* and *Green Pastures*.

But, as Montaigne pointed out, one does not need a vast and imposing theater nor lofty players for the human comedy. On many days the "Living" section of the New Orleans *Times-Picayune,* with its inane columns concerning Anne Dupuy's aquamarine gown seen at the Orléans Club debutante tea and Derrick and Jane Lawson's recent return from the Caribbean, offers nothing essentially different from the weekly *Avalanche* fare, except that there it would have been San Antonio or El Paso, not the Caribbean, from which these darlings of society had returned. Kings and peasants alike sit on their rumps, and the fundamental truths of life are as available in a desert town of five thousand people as they are in Paris or New York. There was time to go into things, and know them well. One played on a small stage, to a small audience, of one's own kind, but that is the sort of theater where a lot of classical drama began and reached its peak. Perhaps some, I confess, deserved a wider hearing. My father liked to quote Gray:

> Full many a gem of purest ray serene
> The dark unfathomed caves of ocean bear.
> Full many a flower is born to blush unseen,
> And waste its sweetness on the desert air.

In any case, the place was not lacking in intrigue. I am no Thomas Wolfe, to make of desire and narrow-mindedness an American epic; my appetites were not so huge as his, nor my resentments so great. But, were I of a mind to do so, I could certainly tell tales that would match anything from the sophisticated suburbia of John Cheever or John Updike.

La Rochefoucauld wrote that hypocrisy is the homage that vice pays to virtue. If so, virtue was certainly honored in that town, by the mask of propriety. True, sin was not made easy, but somehow people managed. The numerous Protestant churches, the chief ones lined up on Avenue D as if to form a rampart against wickedness, represented the standards to which citizens felt they were expected to, and pretended to, adhere. Then the individual vigilance of private citizens constituted another bastion against impropriety. On one occasion, my good mother was told by a Southern Baptist busybody that she was headed for perdition if she didn't mend her ways (what *had* she done?). Tongues wagged liberally (well, no, but facilely). Consider, for instance, the irritation, five years later, of a twenty-year-old back from Rice who was told by her parents that old Mrs. Henry had commented on a certain evening of cards that had lasted until 2 A.M. People had seen to it that occasions for drinking were not numerous; you could get beer at the pool hall, which proper folk never entered, and at the Green Café on the other side of the tracks, or buy a half-pint at the package store, but that was about all. There were movie theaters, of course—the Grenada in town, the Lobo and Twin Peaks drive-ins—but scarcely anything was shown more risqué than *Gigi,* with Maurice Chevalier. In short, even under the cloak of hypocrisy, it was rather difficult to err in the several ways that almost anyone now takes for granted.

That is, in all except one. That one was sex, always available and free, if one doesn't count the occasional costs (to men only, before the egalitarian days) of what is called either courtship or seduction, depending upon one's ostensible intentions and the legal status of the object of one's pursuits. To offset very limited physical possibilities (no matter what eroticists say), sex can be varied by persons. What the high school and college boys were able to accomplish along that line I know from hearsay and observation, not experience. A friend some years later was obliged to return home permanently from a prestigious university in the East because his seduction of—or by—a shopgirl had had consequences; but I think such instances were not frequent, because girls still took pride in their reputations, or at least would have felt shame at being known to be careless of them, and this attitude was bolstered by the practical difficulty, in a town of only three doctors and two drugstores and where everyone knew everyone's parents, of obtaining contraceptive devices. Among married adults, however, some of whom had isolated ranch property or could afford to go to El Paso for a *rendez-vous,* there were clearly fewer inhibitions. Remarks about such as Jimmie Anne Jones, who was seeing on the sly a well-known businessman, and Elvira Holmes, who had a long-running affair with a Fort Davis rancher, furnished the conversational meat at many gatherings, no less substantial for being served in low tones. Elvira was not involved even in an adulterous affair; it was just that the rancher didn't seem to want to marry her, and yet they took trips together. Hypocrisy, I said—for some of those who judged had erred themselves; but not only hypocrisy, since the erring also believed in the very institution of marriage that they were violating.

Then, there was crime, mostly petty, pathetic even. The year we arrived, the cashier of the bank disappeared suddenly, and irregularities were found. He shot himself before he could be arrested. It was discovered that he had invested the money in tanks on some ranch property in Presidio County that wasn't even his. (A tank, in West Texas, can be a concrete structure, or simply a depression surrounded by earthen dikes to create a watering trough for cattle; in either case, the water is pumped by windmills.) Another instance involved a widow, whose first husband had similarly killed himself, after what disappointments I do not know. When an attractive man from Arkansas came to town and courted her, he seemed an ideal father for her young son, and she helped him arrange for a loan and other favors, whereupon he left with the cash and some of her possessions. Some years later, the college president himself left abruptly, having perhaps misspent moneys that belonged to the people of Texas. Too, there were occasional drunken brawls and knife fights, notably in the balcony of the Grenada Theater, where the Mexicans sat, and rumors of incest, especially in Marathon. Sheriff Weber put some of the offenders in jail, an old structure appended to the courthouse. It wasn't a very nice place; but, as Constable Billy Pat McGuiness said at a later date when a reporter from ABC's *20/20* made the same observation about the Terlingua jail, "We don't put nice people in it."

With drug smuggling and more potent weapons, crime has doubtless increased since, but old-fashioned assault is still around.

A year or so ago, the Houston *Chronicle* carried a story about a case pending in county court, involving an attorney named Joe Delaney and old Dr. Hill, who practiced medicine there for forty years and is now more than four-score years old. First, Dr. Hill was convicted of punching the fifty-seven-year-old lawyer (who is also a part-time science fiction writer); then the latter was filmed spitting on the doctor's window; finally Delaney was accused of having sent his adversary flying through a plate-glass window. Delaney, while claiming in court papers that the physician had tried to run him down with his car, made his case somewhat shakier by threatening publicly the district attorney, who then filed a felony retaliation charge against him. The whole matter, which is not yet settled, has now taken on political overtones, and, as friends recently told me, what the *Chronicle* called Alpine's "Epoch of Weirdness" (did it mean *epic?*) may drag on for years, against a backdrop of power struggles in which the various factions throw the Delaney-Hill controversy in each other's faces.

I think that some of these incidents can be explained by what seemed to be an unusual number of misfits in Alpine. Were they just more visible there? I think not. So far from everywhere, and offering few chances for substantial achievement and gain to those who carefully plan out their lives, the town acted as an equivalent of the frontier, to which were drawn those who did not fit in elsewhere, sometimes running from something, or ready to take their chances with anything or anyone else. In his entirely honorable way, my father was one of these, not, unlike some, because he could not maintain an established family life (in that way, no one was more settled, more reliable), but through his restlessness and his inability to play the game of success. You can imagine that some of these misfits—washouts from other institutions, marginally qualified professional and management people—succeeded in getting on at the college, the smallest and least prestigious in the Texas system, where doctorates in education seemed to be the rule and to have a Ph.D. from anywhere other than the University of Texas made a faculty member truly exceptional. Preachers of the churches *not* on Avenue D were likely to be in this category of the ill-adapted; some brought with them a record of failures, if not immorality, and several left as quickly as they had appeared.

For some years at least, my father was quite happy to make a life in the desert, to which, in earlier times, thinkers and what are currently called "weirdos," including John the Baptist and Saint Jerome, were drawn. For him, it corresponded perhaps to his refusal of the world too much with us; and certainly the simplicity of life in an isolated town was salubrious for him, although it could not totally keep him from melancholy (he would sometimes sit for a long while, his head buried in his hands, listening to pieces by Mozart—the late ones—or Beethoven). He worked summers in Colorado (giving driver's examinations and lessons), taught for a year at the high school, and then was hired at the college, thanks to the student mentioned before, who, having taken Father's high school courses, persuaded his own father, the college president (*not* the one who left abruptly) to hire him there. No matter that he had only a master's degree: the president took seriously his responsibility of providing as much good teaching as possible, needed especially by the unsophisticated students of Sul Ross; and anyway, Father knew more than one of his colleagues, who, despite his Ph.D., expressed one day his surprise at learning that Ireland was an island.

My parents finally bought a modest house, near the Fort Davis highway, looking out over a vast cactus field (called "pasture" and, beyond, amazingly, "golf course"), with the hills bordering it. The house was on a sizeable lot, grassed and fenced at the front, and, in the back, divided into two yards. The inner one similarly had grass, maintained—given the annual rainfall of about seven inches—at tremendous cost of labor and well water. The outer was left as nature had arranged it, with a few wild grasses, cholla cactuses, and dust. Later my father bought trees through a mail-order catalogue—apple, maple, and especially peach—all of which he watered assiduously, and splendid crops of fruit appeared year after year. A recent visit revealed that, while the house, long since sold, has fallen into a state of blight, at least the full and stately trees, whose roots now water themselves from deep sources, still oppose their ample shade to the terrific desert sun.

Yet despite his own adjustment to the place, which lasted not much more than ten years but at least was beneficial, my father had no intention of letting me make my life in Alpine. The first summer we were there, Mother was assigned as a grader to Professor Wilfred S. Dowden, who had come on a visiting appointment, from Rice. His Ph.D. was from the University of North Carolina; eventually he became a major authority on Thomas Moore and other Romantic figures. (The Dowdens' choice to spend the summer in Alpine reflected two things: the abysmally low salaries even the most reputable institutions paid then, and the near-absence of air conditioning in Houston. If you are going to be hot, at least it's better to be dry.) Will suggested that I apply to Rice, a school so distant that we would not otherwise have thought about it. As the only major institution in Texas not connected to either state or church, it was known as the atheist school, though he was himself a Presbyterian and many others on the faculty, as I remember them, ascribed honor to the Lord. (Doubtless the fact that there I took up French, associated with lax morality, made the image worse in some people's minds.) To him and his wife I am indebted for this simple suggestion and their support, although not determinism, but determination, would have led me to find *some* way to attend a university other than Sul Ross, no matter what the obstacles.

When I graduated one year later from Alpine High, I was barely seventeen and had gone to high school for only three and a half years, because of a strange arrangement in Denver whereby I had skipped a semester. No one in the school office seemed to realize so, since Denver summer school credits gave me sufficient hours for graduation. It would be supposed now in college admissions offices with which I am familiar that someone coming from a small high school in a benighted area such as West Texas, who had never traveled much farther east than San Antonio, would find the university difficult; "adjustment problems" would be predicted. (As a friend of my husband's said when introduced to me, "If you're from Texas, how can you be so cultured?") But this turned out not to be so; the staff at Alpine High was able and the curriculum solid, my parents had made me literate, and I was a reader, and determined to read more, as well as write.

The change from small western town to a major city and a superior, if small, university was crucial, however. Paradoxically, I find myself justifying now the need to get away, at the same time that I have argued for the desert as a place to see life clearly and—almost—see it whole. In some ways, of course, I have never left, and the caliche-strewn earth of the cemetery south of town, barely shaded by scattered funereal cypresses, holds a part of me just as it contains my parents. Many of my tastes were molded there, notably, among mundane ones, for Tex-Mex enchiladas with red chile sauce, onions, and cheese, and for Mexican architecture, especially patios with cactuses, and Spanish ballads about border towns. I can still appreciate something of the *mañana* way of managing life, which may have appealed to my father also and is not without an element of grace. But, on the threshold of adulthood, the adventures of the heart and mind need a wider and more populous cultural arena. Though I loved wildly the desert and skylines of the Big Bend, when I first took the train for Houston, it was different from the trip to San Antonio: this time the departure implied a search for change, the "leading out" that is the true meaning of education, which would involve not only study at the university and in the foreign, yet fraternal world of France, but the affective adventures of love and failure and grief. So I left; and I applaud those others who were able to do so. Perhaps, despite the distance time and experience disclose in the self, it is they, and I, who know the place best, seeing it through the powerful glass of memory, which concentrates on things a light that almost burns. I can imagine the western range now at evening, the Twin Peaks, symmetrical and harmonious, and their jagged companions falling into rich shadow when the sun props itself in swollen indolence at their crest. Or I picture the cactus-pink reflections in the east, as I climb onto the Sunset Limited bound for Houston, leaving the undivided desert of the self for the contradictions of adulthood, and both the burden and the flowering of life.

Leaving for Good

*W*riters seem particularly drawn to departures, whether they thrive on them or suffer from them (hence perhaps thrive indirectly). Is it because they sense that each poem, each novel, each art object is phenomenologically whole, a radical separation from what precedes, with its own opening and closure, for which their vital experience must provide a parallel? Or because, as Gide put it, "Perception begins with a change in sensation, hence the necessity of travel?" Rather than to those who stayed put (but is there any modern artist to rival the philosopher Kant, who barely left Königsberg?), I am drawn to the great travelers among modern writers—Gide himself, Henri Michaux (who was also given to a more dangerous means of displacement, hallucinatory drugs), Malraux, Beauvoir, and my friend the poet Jean-Claude Renard, among the French writers whose works I know well; even Proust managed to tear himself away from his social life and his habits to go to Venice. And then there are the *exilés,* of whom Camus, with his exemplary title *Exile and the Kingdom,* is the most haunting.

My own experience with displacement, generally on a modest scale, has taken place through family uprootings, travel, change consciously sought, and the vicissitudes of love and career, all entangled with each other. I came honestly to my itchy feet. Since I was born on this side of the Atlantic and am not of American-Indian blood, it follows that every one of my lines of ancestors, at one generation or another, came to this continent as immigrants. On the maternal side, a Van Pelt family settled in New York in the seventeenth century. To this Dutch line was added eventually the English name Stanforth—my mother's. On my father's side, before the Revolutionary War four Hill brothers came to the colonies from England. When the rebellion broke out, three, of loyalist sentiment, returned to England. A fourth, William, remained, joining the revolutionary armies. (This fact may explain the number of rebellious and hard-headed Hills I have known.) William must have been the great-great-grandfather of my own grandfather, Edward Curtis Hill.

The latter, born in Illinois in 1863, went to Colorado and became a journalist in Saguache, where he met my grandmother, a Miss Elliott. She was herself an exemplary case of departure, having gone by train and then stagecoach from her home in Montreal to the Rockies, where it was hoped (with cause, it turned out) that she could survive and not succumb to tuberculosis or other diseases, like most of her family. My grandfather then went to medical school and spent a very long life in Colorado as a physician, professor of chemistry, and occasional writer; but he and my grandmother were greatly given to travel and took lengthy trips abroad, including a ten-week circumnavigation of Africa and a tour of South America. In 1937 the Baltimore *Sun* for December 3 carried an article about their departure on that date, aboard the Baltimore Mail Line's *City of Hamburg,* on the first leg of a round-the-world cruise, which lasted six months. It took them, among other places, to Japan, where my grandmother made friends, with whom she corresponded until the war and my uncle Jack's death in the Pacific put an end to her amicable feeling for the Japanese.

On my mother's side, families moved, generation by generation, from New York and Virginia to Ohio, Kentucky, and Missouri or whatever was then called the West, which, as it progressively became the penultimate rather than the ultimate frontier, led to my Stanforth grandparents' arrival in Colorado in the late nineteenth century. (The later settling of both Stanforth and Hill brothers in California completed the transcontinental movement of the families.) In many of these cases, I am confident, those who left their previous homes and families knew—in the first sense of the expression—and hoped—in the second, literal sense—that they were leaving for good.

Things have changed; we have become travelers, not migrants. As a small child, I accompanied my parents, by car or train, to Colorado Springs, Woodland Park, Bailey, where my grandmother had a cabin, Yampa, Lake City, and Ouray, all in Colorado, and to towns in Wyoming; later, there were annual trips to camp—the Flying-G Ranch—and the early family displacements to Arizona and Texas, including the permanent move to Alpine, in the Big Bend country. Sometimes I said good-bye to places and friends to which I was attached; but I recall no time in those days when I was reluctant to leave, metaphysical anguish not yet having attached itself to the idea of separation, and the prospect of the new outweighing any sense of rootedness. This refusal to tie myself even to what I had enjoyed may have been simply vitality, or the sense of projection toward the future that is integral to the human experience (and which helps explain why youth seems quintessentially human); or perhaps it was partly a reluctance to become typed in any fashion, to be identified with a group, a mode of life—as long, that is, as the self had not elected and internalized it. I was then still a tomboy, most comfortable in jeans, a leather jacket, and shirts bought in the boys' department, and I refused to curl my hair, long and black, according to the fashion of the time, wearing it instead quite straight. (These obstinacies led to some words between me and my mother, who feared doubtless for my future and was embarrassed when I appeared in front of her friends, shirt not tucked in, hair cropped at the forehead in a short bang and the rest falling lank over my shoulders.)

None of these trips took me away from the West, whose vast perspectives are offset by considerable cultural homogeneity, and thus they might seem inconsequential; but the uprootings may have molded me. Two years after we settled in Alpine came my first watershed departure, at seventeen—alone, for Houston, still Texas but no longer the West. This time, I was dressed in a suit and shoes with heels—hand-me-downs from my stylish Aunt Mollie in Los Angeles—and my hair was in a more respectable, if eccentric, style (long braids over the head). I got on the Sunset Limited one evening in September, to ride all night in the coach. The car was full of soldiers (this was the year after war broke out in Korea); I vaguely remember my mother warning me about them at some earlier point. At the other end of the ride lay the Rice Institute, which I had never seen, and, in a sense, the rest of my life. Waking after a few hours of neck-twisting sleep, I saw more green than I had ever imagined—green in the ditches, green in the trees and fields, green in the vines that added a superfluity of leaves to the trees and reclaimed the telephone poles for nature, almost transforming the wires themselves into vegetation. When I stepped down onto the platform in Houston, something else struck me, not visible or audible, a sensation of being hit in the face and smothered; it was, I learned, Gulf Coast humidity, to be with me for roughly the next ten years and, in its even more intense New Orleans form, part of my life since 1968.

That this departure for Rice was "leaving for good" in the metaphoric sense is certain, for, even though I would return for Christmas and summer vacations, it constituted the moment when, astraddle girlhood and womanhood, I moved like a reserve soldier from behind the front lines of family and home—a home that is constituted by time as well as place and thus holds the heart doubly—to put myself thenceforth in the direct line of life. It was also good that I was leaving. It is not just fatalism that leads me to say so. (My fatalism I get from my father, who preached caution to me and practiced it himself, yet was willing to ride with my cousin in an old school bus over a primitive road laid across an abandoned railroad trestle on Corona Pass in Colorado, with a drop of a couple hundred feet below.) A backward-looking determinism that turns "what has been" into "what had to be" denies freedom by creating a pseudo-historical necessity, which becomes identified, through a popular dialectics almost as powerful as the Marxist one, with the good. Not everything that was, was good.

But that departure was. Inexperienced and unsophisticated I doubtless was—the city equivalent of a tenderfoot—but I was self-reliant and determined. The sort of rigorous regimen imposed at Rice—few electives, fast-paced courses taught by professors of the old school, including a number from Europe—was not beneficial to all, but I liked and profited from everything (except possibly the laboratory in Chemistry 120, despite, not because of, which I did well in the course). Most of us were what are now called "grinds"; those who were not generally failed. It never occurred to me that brains might be viewed as a hindrance for a woman; the fact that I discovered so only years later may suggest that I was socially retarded, but also reflects the tone of the place. Despite heavy demands, we had abundant good times, and there were men in my life every year, since I had stopped being one of the boys and become one of the girls.

Because there were no residence halls on campus for women, the Rice authorities had turned apartments in a complex they owned into quarters for those few girls from out of town. The first year I lived in a small apartment with four other students, thereafter, with three, all of us underfoot to the others constantly but getting along. Food was our responsibility. My companions often cooked ("cooking" being for one of them opening a can of Beenie-Weenie and a Pepsi), and sometimes I joined them, but more often ate at the drugstore, Weldon's Cafeteria, or the men's commons on campus, where the others too had dining privileges but only I was stubborn enough and free enough of self-consciousness to exercise them. (Also, I am literal-minded; if the sign says "Stop" I stop, and if I am told that the dining hall is for me as well as others, I eat there. It may appear to be a strange trait for a poet, but is not really, since it comes from a tremendous respect for language and its potentialities for conveying truths.)

Across a U-shaped courtyard from us lived mostly untenured faculty members, including a couple of strange mathematicians and a young and very gifted poet, James Dickey. One of my roommates was his student in English 100. She retained from the class chiefly the image of an eccentric who would place his chair on the table and then climb onto both, whence he taught by way of chatting amiably. It was believed that he had some sort of optical device for gazing across the courtyard into our windows. Many years later, when I introduced myself to him after he had given a reading in Virginia, he said, "Oh yes, I remember you, I used to look at you through my glass."

Traveling during those undergraduate years was not limited to twice-a-year trips to and from Houston. The summer I was eighteen, my mother took me to Kansas and Missouri to visit relatives of hers. At Dalhart, where my father had driven us, we got on the Rock Island line. I had a new green dress, casual but proper, and a new hairstyle, the roommates having succeeded in persuading me to cut my idiosyncratic plaits. We stopped in Newton, Kirk-wood, and other places I have forgotten. In fact, Mother forbade me to remember one of them. It was outside a town somewhere in eastern Missouri. Through mud nearly up to the axles, we were taken by mule-wagon to the farm of a distant relation. I understood then why my cousin Raymond used to tease our great-aunt Mag, who was from there, by asking her whether it was true that all Missourians had webbed feet. Food was copious—heavy farm cooking in steaming bowls that covered a nearly groaning board—but the accommodations were primitive, including somewhat musty mattresses, an old box phone affixed to the wall, and a privy standing in a moat of the same mud through which the mules had brought us. Mother was so embarrassed, less directly—after all, these were upright, hardworking folk of the sort she had known as a young woman in Colorado and Wyoming—than through me, sensing my lack of ease, that she made me promise never to speak of it. Her shade will forgive me now.

My father met us at the train in Denver and drove us back to Alpine. Some weeks later, I left again, to meet a friend in New Mexico. She and I had won scholarships to some Danforth-supported camp near Muskogee, Michigan. We took the Rock Island to Chicago, arriving late because of breakdowns, and then a filthy old coach of the Baltimore and Ohio line. I did not like the camp in every respect—too much preaching and Pollyanna sentimentalism, not enough critical thinking, to my mind—but Chicago, the first classic American city I had seen, was memorable. I remember carrying a huge duffle bag on my shoulders between one station and another, and staring like the small-town girl that was part of me at things my mother had described (she had attended the university there). On the return trip, we rode to Tucumcari, New Mexico; then I took a bus and the Texas & Pacific to Pecos, and somehow got home from there. None of these passenger lines exists anymore. Those who have not crossed the wheat plains of Kansas and Texas in mid-July, in a coach moving slowly or not at all, the fumes and dust drifting through the window, the waves of heat distorting fields and sky, might ask themselves whether they know summer fully.

The classic departure for educated American youth in both the previous century and this one is expatriation to Europe. After taking my master's degree, I was fortunate enough to have a *Wanderjahr,* or rather a year mostly of study, at a time when I could profit from it well. France was for me, and remains, an intellectual home, the repository of centuries of culture to which something in me lays claim. When I arrived, it still greatly resembled its prewar condition, having not yet undergone the Americanization of the 1960s, 1970s, and beyond, a transformation that, in the eyes of many, has ruined it and yet is a sign of a prosperity that, God knows, the French needed. I took the train to New York, then the little *Flandre* of the French Line to Le Havre, and spent the next eight months reading, taking courses, trying to keep warm in unheated lecture halls and a barely warmed rented room, where I wrote wearing gloves, and coughing, since I had caught a dreadful cold that turned into bronchitis.

The spring and summer finally came, with trips to Italy and Greece to see the great cities of antiquity, and to much of the rest of Europe. I traveled with a fellow American, a lovely girl, with whom my friendship has endured, though she returned to her native South Dakota. A former contestant in a state beauty pageant, she was a true blonde, with large brown eyes. Whereas those we met recognized the name of Texas, she could never get anyone to understand where she was from; she finally resorted to stretching the truth so far as to say it was "near Chicago." At Easter, we took a ship from Marseilles to Naples—or rather, were supposed to. Somehow, we missed the thing, and after a memorable dispute with officials in the port, whose incompetence may not have been unrelated to the contretemps, we had to catch up with the ship in Genoa. Of the rest of the voyage I recall only that people somehow mistook us for movie stars—an error we felt obliged to rectify. In Naples, I had my first shower in months, the rented rooms where I had stayed in France having no such facilities and, in one case, not even hot water. In June we sailed to Piraeus, then crossed Greece and Yugoslavia by rail in a primitive coach we shared with peasants, chickens, and very sinister-looking policemen. Everywhere, my blonde companion drew admiring looks and often unwelcome solicitations—so that at the end of the summer we could have drawn over the map of Europe a *Carte du Tendre,* each capital marked with a broken heart.

By going to France I was, in a sense, following my father's sister Mary. She had sailed in late spring of 1939 to spend the summer at the arts school in Fontainebleau, studying piano with Robert Casadesus and Nadia Boulanger. By the end of her course of study, war had been declared and she was unable to return as she had planned. Finally she got passage on a ferry to Folkestone and then what may have been the last ship to carry travelers to New York. In some ways I was also going back to a European home that, through atavism and culture, was already mine before I was born. These cultural affinities are not sheer fancy. When my father first visited England in the late 1950s, he fell in love with it as with few other things—as though responding to something deep in his genes. After my parents had spent the academic year 1962–1963 first at Balliol College and then in Kent, where he taught American literature in Oxford's extension program, he felt that he could not live unless he could settle there. Perhaps he was right; I sometimes think that his premature death was caused partly by my mother's refusal to cast her lot there permanently.

Since those first trips of undergraduate and postgraduate years, I have done a great deal of traveling, in Europe, to Canada, Mexico, and the Caribbean, to every state in the U.S. except Hawaii. Rarely do I take work with me; work belongs in its own setting—the familiar library where one can put one's hands on the desired books simply by turning a corner and letting one's eyes follow an accustomed path to the shelves, or the comfortable home study, a heteroclitic arrangement of books and furnishings but serving, by its strange disorder, the order of reflection and writing. Travel is, indeed, its own serious business; it calls for commitment and a fallow mind, not just a camera, ready for impressions. It demonstrates, and adds to, one's availability for experiences and, by that token, should be favored by the old and young alike. When my grandmother Hill, in her late eighties, decided to go to San Francisco to visit her eldest son there, someone criticized the project as risky. Her answer was that she would just as soon die on a Union Pacific train as anywhere else. Montaigne and others have considered travel the school of life. But in a sense it is life itself, accelerated, intensified, multiplied; and thus its effects are akin to those of love—a fact that allows vacationers to take for powerful sentiment a passing erotic attraction, which benefits from their enhanced vitality as well as from exotic settings and anonymity. The opposite of the strange inclination to "wait home quietly to die" (to quote a phrase mocked by Beauvoir in *Pyrrhus et Cinéas*), travel is almost the denial of death, allowing us to imagine that final departure as a voyage, only a voyage to nowhere . . .

The peculiar thing, in my case, is that I am married to a man who does not like to travel. Common among New Orleanians is the attitude "Why leave?—I'm already there." But in his case the disinclination is deeper: mostly, he fears all change like the plague. Going to Korea and back with the Marines was more than enough to exhaust his few mental resources in that area. Our wedding trip—that journey following the ceremony that seems integral to the new departure of marriage—consisted of a long drive back to New Orleans from the courthouse of the City and County of Denver, a trip that had to be made since circumstances had led to our marrying in Colorado; otherwise, we would have been married here and probably would have gone no farther than the French Quarter for our honeymoon. On the drive down, we stayed in ordinary motels at best and, in Bunkie, Louisiana, in a shabby place called the Kent Court, since torn down (deservedly), in whose musty, roach-infested cottages and spoon-shaped mattresses even the traveling salesman of crude jokes would not care to cast his lot for the night.

When we do leave, since my husband's rocking chair and other domestic paraphernalia are not portable, he does his best to take his habits with him. So his first concern is to establish a new routine, composed of the slightest elements—the same café for breakfast (the same table if possible), going for the morning paper, listening to news with a bourbon-and-soda at 5:30, and so on. As I write this we are about to leave by car for Lake Tahoe, and the best moments for him will doubtless be those when, settled in a lodge for a week, he can transform it by his habits into a sort of home. (When he finally agreed to our daughter's urging that, after twelve years without one, we again make *some* sort of family trip, he was given the choice of destination, and decided on that lovely spot, which he had once admired. No matter that it is 2,200 miles away and that he really likes neither the desert nor the arid mountains through which we must pass. It turns out that he thought that only something so remote would satisfy the vagabond in us.)

Of my numerous travels in recent years, the most memorable is a trip in the summer of 1981, when I escorted my dear old aunts and my daughter to Europe on the *QE2*. Aunt Mary was then almost eighty-seven, somewhat deaf, and lame from an accident in Athens in which a wild-bucking motorcyclist had run her down on the sidewalk, but she liked being on shipboard and was a great sport. Her sister Flora, who, at nearly eighty, weighed scarcely more and looked like a leprechaun, was just as delightful. They charmed the French, who love women of any age, even if they can speak only rudimentary French (their case, since both had lost the facility they had acquired as young women) or none at all. Flora would drink Ouzo, when we could get it, or Kir or a wonderful Burgundian wine we bought in pitchers in Dijon, and then she would hang spoons on her nose, gesture imaginatively in order to communicate with the waiters, and end up fascinating everyone. In Vézelay, where I was interviewing the military writer Jules Roy, we had tea with Roy and his wife, Tatiana, every afternoon and an occasional lunch or dinner. I swear that, by the time we left, "Julius" was half in love with them both.

They were pleased with Cherbourg, where we landed, and especially Bayeux, Saint-Malo, and Mont Saint-Michel; they took to Orléans and Vézelay as warmly as our friends there welcomed them; they admired Dijon, where Flora climbed the tower of Philip the Good, with its hundreds of steps, in order to look out over the splendid tile roofs of the city. That evening, she fell, apparently during a struggle to pull the massive curtains in the hotel room—or did her legs, not surprisingly, just give way under her? During the rest of the journey, she limped worse than Mary, hobbling around on my arm or using a tripod cane we bought when we arrived in Paris.

Leaving Europe proved to be the hardest part. We were to return on the ship, which was to sail from Southampton. Having decided that we wanted to see a bit of London, we sent the bags ahead from Paris and got tickets on the boat train for Boulogne. The Saint-Lazare station, which we had difficulty reaching because it is very hard to persuade a French taxi driver to take four people plus their hand baggage, was packed as for a riot; the train was just as crowded. The other passengers in the compartment were English returning from a holiday. A father and his son, their extended legs crisscrossed so as to create traps for anyone else, watched in silence as I struggled to load onto the *filets* (wire racks) all our hand baggage, while the train lurched out of the city. Later, when the sullen pair had stepped out, Flora asked whether she should offer them some of the delicious cakes my friend Maggie Gillet had given us for the trip (fortunately, since delays were compounded by delays and we did not get a bite of lunch till around 3 : 30, on the ferry; those who, like me, want their meals served like clockwork will imagine the mood into which this prolonged fast had put me). Hesitating at being mean-spirited but reluctant to reward callousness, I said no.

For two days in London we saw what we could—National Gallery, Tate Gallery, Westminster Abbey, Saint Paul's, I believe— two lame old women, a child just days short of her tenth birthday, and I. Then I went to get tickets for the train to Southampton. The clerk's curt phrase through the wicket is still sharp in my memory: "Madam, that ship is leaving from Cherbourg." A strike at Southampton had caused the change, unbeknownst to us, before we had crossed the Channel. Still, Cunard was not going to abandon us; with several hundred other passengers, we were put onto a dusty old train for Portsmouth, whence we were to transfer to a Norwegian ferry bound for Cherbourg. The bags had caught up with us, of course, or we with them—minus one, which had disappeared while supposedly under a porter's watchful eye at the hotel in London. With the heavy luggage handed over to *QE2* workers, but two or three other pieces dangling from my shoulders as I pushed one of the aunts in a wheelchair and clung to the child with my other hand, we were the very last of some seven hundred Cunard passengers to board the ferry.

This vessel had been designed for a few hundred cross-Channel travelers; the number of passengers had more than doubled, and the amount of baggage quadrupled. By the time we reached the decks and public rooms, not a place was left to sit, scarcely any to stand. If the boat had hit an obstacle in the fog, we would all have died like drowned sheep. The "lous" were awash in water and probably urine, and the dining room soon proved utterly inadequate for the many who had not eaten since breakfast. The crossing was to take five hours. In the stairs, I inquired of an officer where I could find seats for two old ladies. "I'm sure, Madam, that's none of my business" was his reply. Fortunately a French family, spying us finally and understanding our plight, moved some luggage and made their children give us seats; I remain grateful to these anonymous Samaritans. Finally, at midnight, again on French soil, we finished making our way through the customs hall at Cherbourg and onto the ship.

It was the aunts' last, weary look at the continent of their forefathers. In 1986 we were planning to return to visit Paris, Vézelay, and Navarre, which Aunt Flora had picked from her reading. Unfortunately, by summertime one of them had departed this life for a greater journey, and the other would soon follow. Since that first, and last, European tour with them, I have gone back, but feel bereft of their presence in France, where we had shared the exhilaration of difference—just as in England, alone, I cannot quite see through my father's eyes.

I wonder whether in each case those who would not live to return to a cherished spot felt, as they left, that they were saying farewell forever. There are moments when it seems to me that *any* change of place, no matter how attractive, is paid for by the fear of separation and death. We moderns can no longer be migrants, I have said, since there is hardly a frontier left except the moon and Mars, and most of the dangers of leaving have disappeared (although white-knuckle flyers, of which I am not one, might argue otherwise); but division and departure and the sense of the *irré-médiable* are still inscribed in our very selves. Good-byes are often highly ambivalent, and the images—now mostly cinematographic and literary, but known by all—of a smile or kiss through a train window, or handkerchiefs waving their unspoken farewell on deck and on shore, while pregnant with suggestions of good fortune and adventure, also conjure up anticipatory loss. Yet, if you study the faces at airports, as families are separating, and even more at bus stations, where drifters and those down on their luck try out new departures, you can still detect—among the anxieties, the hopes mixed with sadness and a sense of failure and estrangement—the signs of the necessary myth of a new life, which, one way or another, brought us where we now are and surrounds, like an atmosphere, the creature who walks with the knowledge that, sooner or later, he will be leaving for good.

Cherry Time

For many people, men and women alike, cherry time, the season when life is in full bloom, comes around age twenty. (The phrase "cherry time" is from a French song—a song of the 1871 Commune, but concerned less with politics and revolution than with the vision of a summer of love and the vitality of youth and happiness, when "the sun is in the heart.") It is a time to seize the day, for, as the aria in Massenet's *Manon* puts it, "We will not always be twenty." For me, cherry time came somewhat tardily, like a delayed summer after a cool, prolonged spring marked by late frosts; but—as though the blossom and the fruit had appeared on the tree at the same time—the flowering proved to be followed by a quick maturity, when the fruits of time and the mind ripened well. Or so it seems now, retrospectively. In any case, the people, work, travels, places, and events associated with one's summer remain keen in the mind, lit with bright sunshine and a vitality that doubtless was less in them than in us. Or was it? Sometimes the genius of place (to use Michel Butor's phrase) seems real and active, and settings, events, and experiences fit extraordinarily, as if instinct led us to the place and the life that will be most propitious. Yes, Virginia, there is a Virginia, a place for the summer of life, one that bears different names according to one's experience, but for me is indeed the Commonwealth that reaches from the Potomac to Hampton Roads, from the Atlantic to the Cumberland Gap and Kentucky and Tennessee—the original West.

When I moved from Texas permanently, it was to take a position at Sweet Briar College, located in the countryside on the eastern slope of the Blue Ridge. My acquaintance with the eastern states was very limited—short interviews at Sweet Briar and Randolph-Macon Woman's College, and brief stops in Washington, New York, and St. Louis (if you will concede that the latter city can be "back East," as we said in the Rockies). Thus I had almost no familiarity with the Atlantic region and particularly not with Virginia speech, architecture, and food, which proved to be very different from what I had known. This is not to say that different mores always disconcerted me: after all, I had lived in France; but one *expects* a foreign nation to be strange—this was in my own country.

The summer before my arrival, I had been in France on an American Council of Learned Societies grant. After a brief trip by plane to California and then visits in Texas, I left Houston in a terrific rainstorm that stretched eastward for a considerable distance. Those who call the central South home will not, I hope, begrudge me the comment that the rain was not the only tedious part: the drive had little to recommend it until I reached the Appalachians. By the time I was in the "southwest"—the corner of Virginia that lies under West Virginia—I was in love with the scenery. The flowing mountain outlines, so much more gently contoured than my desert Rockies and generously clothed in seamless vegetation of a soft dark green, followed me like a surf for hundreds of miles. Without the strong contrasts of the real Southwest, the light was nonetheless bright, golden against strata of green fields, green slopes, dark summits, and blue sky.

Something else struck me also—the eighteenth- and nineteenth-century styles and the dark brick of old houses, small factories, and Main Street buildings in the villages and towns through which I passed, on Route 11 and then (via 460) Route 29. In Texas there is almost no old brick, unless you count adobe, and the only native styles deserving the term *old* are Spanish mission architecture and homestead cabins. It was, I believe, shortly after crossing the James River in Lynchburg, along whose banks stands a rampart of vine-covered walls of red brick, almost as dark as the water, that I reached a little crossroads whose name has escaped me and which I cannot find on the map. It consisted of a roadhouse and tavern, a general store, and an old shop that appeared to be right out of the nineteenth century, which displayed hubcaps and other accessories for motorized vehicles but surely still had old harness equipment in a back room.

South of Amherst (nothing but a village), I located the college and learned that, since lodging was scarce, faculty took what they were given in order of priority. I was assigned to quarters in a house owned by the Faulconers. The name was common in the county, appearing on the gasoline station and general store; I was told that there was kinship between them and the Falkners of Mississippi, but cannot confirm it. The house was on a knoll overlooking Route 29; beyond ran the main line of the Southern Railway. Dorothy Faulconer and her husband had the downstairs; I lived above, with a good view. But during that year he was very ill with a brain tumor; the atmosphere was not cheery.

I had chosen Sweet Briar over a major state university, one closer to Texas and with a graduate program in French. From the academic perspective, it was the wrong decision—but, precisely, that is merely an academic point of view. The friend who advised me to go to Virginia was, I realized later, nostalgic for a certain type of campus atmosphere that he associated, not entirely accurately, with the prestigious women's colleges of the Southeast. He meant well, of course. What is required, in my eyes, for an atmosphere to be "intellectual"—assuming the adjective has meaning—is a strong commitment to knowledge and ideas, and a life consistent with this commitment. The term did not fit the college I found, which had an elitist tone, no doubt about it, but only socially. Many students came from wealthy families, and some boarded their horses nearby; many would, after two years, return to their home cities to become debutantes and then finish up at the University of Texas or Ole Miss or Newcomb College. The academic performance was solid but nothing more, and the number of faculty members involved in research or writing—looking beyond the confines of the lecture hall or laboratory—was small. How could it be otherwise? The administration placed no emphasis on such pursuits, and it showed. During most of the first term, I taught sixteen hours a week (rather than the thirteen I had expected—already a considerable assignment) and had five preparations, the illness of another professor having created a void that I had to help fill. The library did not provide what I would have needed to carry on my reading of modern French political novels.

Cherry Time

As for those in chemistry and so on, what could they do in laboratories that were intended for demonstration, not investigation? What is surprising is that in my few months there I was able, amidst the handicaps, to write both critical articles and poetry.

Despite the absence of what I have called an intellectual spirit, the sense of community at Sweet Briar was real, but not suitable for me—or rather, I was not quite suited to it, since I came from a different culture from that of most of the faculty, many of whom had grown up in Virginia or at least the Atlantic region, and some of whom had the characteristic accent either of the Tidewater, with its "hoose" (house), or of the mountains, and were as parochial in their way as I must have been in mine. The Boxwood Inn, a lunch place run by the college, illustrated this provincialism. The main dish at lunch seemed usually to be "ham biscuits"—bits of ham stuffed into dry biscuit layers—something I had never seen before (my shortcoming) and the manager and many patrons apparently found delicious (theirs). This manager was the same person who referred to a copy of one of Gauguin's Tahiti scenes, which hung incongruously near the cash register, as "darkies swimming." The clients were, of course, the same people one taught with, saw at meetings, concerts, and campus movies, and "recreated" with—a life too cloistered, or rather, incestuous, for me.

Moreover, there was a slightly Sapphic quality to the college. Nevertheless, some friendships *were* formed—there were, happily, some men also—and they were good ones. Some of us often played poker together, or drove to Lynchburg to see a movie or go bowling or to Charlottesville for a play or lecture; five of us made a film, *Wild Raspberries,* not merely a parody of Ingmar Bergman's masterpiece. We had campus visits from major writers—Flannery O'Connor, Howard Nemerov—and heard Dickey, Robert Lowell, George Garrett, and others in Charlottesville. Alone or with a close friend, I explored that part of the Blue Ridge, and also went to Washington for theater and music. Since my parents were in England for the year, instead of returning to Texas I visited New York at Thanksgiving, California at Christmas, and Denver for the spring vacation. In some ways the year was a painful one, emotionally, but the time spent in being unhappy, like the time spent on teaching, did not prevent me from writing.

In the spring came an offer to teach at the University of Florida, an offer I accepted without having visited that institution or the state, for, despite the pleasures just noted, I concluded that I would not learn to like Sweet Briar—too isolated, too turned in on itself—and it had become clear that I could not pursue there the type of academic career I wanted; anyhow, my closest friend was leaving for New York. But in June, as I drove down Route 29 toward Georgia and Florida, I took with me not only books, records, and a few household things crammed into the car, but also a love for Virginia that had crystalized around the sumac-fringed roads, drives to Buena Vista, Forks of Buffalo, and Piney River, oyster stew eaten at a roadside place in Amherst, beers with friends or visitors at the Briar Patch on the highway, and the fences and spring-green pastures behind the house, rising toward the distant crests of the Blue Ridge.

I did not, however, suspect that I would return. The return was a matter of sheer chance, that chance which is responsible for so much of what we are and do and which, despite its risks, we should respect and not try to confine or rationalize away entirely. It was embodied in someone I met the following year and who was a Virginian. In Florida, I was not at all unhappy; quite the contrary. My colleagues included excellent young professors in French, Spanish, and English, and teaching graduate courses provided opportunities for extensive research in areas that interested me. The three years I spent there were extremely productive and were filled with the pleasures of friendship, travel, and the arts. Presumably I would have stayed there much longer, had it not been for my friend's decision to settle in Charlottesville. First, we spent a summer there; then I returned for a year to Gainesville; finally I left Florida permanently, to take a position at Mary Baldwin College, in Staunton, across the Ridge from the university designed by Mr. Jefferson. Strange comings and goings—for they were fraught with anxiety and uncertainty, and the marriage that might have ended the latter did not take place. To make a change of this magnitude for someone you love is at once the height of folly and the most reasonable thing in the world.

It was during this second period in the Old Dominion that my acquaintance with it became both broader and deeper, making me a permanent Virginophile. Mary Baldwin was much more appealing to me than Sweet Briar. Although Calvinists are not known for their cheerfulness, it was perhaps good Presbyterian virtues that made the college a more pleasant place: snobbishness was frowned upon and there was a spirit of moral and intellectual community that was comforting. Architecturally, the campus, which overlooks the main business streets of Staunton, is lovely; the fact that it is cramped on a hillside in town makes it, perhaps, seem more in touch with the world, and the buildings, of a pale yellow, with white columns, look both historical and vital, blending well with the surrounding houses and church. I made good friends among the faculty, and for the first time learned truly to appreciate a dean. Despite the endless excursions to be detailed shortly, I was able to write, using the University of Virginia library in order to finish a book, having success in placing my poems, and accumulating a store of notes and drafts of poems that served me for some years thereafter.

Living right in the center of the Shenandoah Valley, between the Blue Ridge and the Shenandoah Mountains, I could see from my office window exquisitely balanced landscapes. Moreover, I had only to drive a few miles in any direction to have these prospects multiplied, both by the sheer numbers of the mountains and by the changing perspectives afforded by the highways and country roads, which ran down the broad valley and twisted narrowly between the adjoining ridges and hills. To the east were Rockfish Gap and Afton Mountain, where Route 250 meets the Skyline Drive, arriving from the north, and the Blue Ridge Parkway, running to the south. To the northeast—the direction the mountain chains and roads run—were a string of historic towns along Massanutten Mountain, an impressive ridge rising from the valley. To the west was a sparsely settled area, including Highland County, where the roads reached altitudes over 4,200 feet, and Bath County, with its chain of eighteenth- and nineteenth-century spas, where old bathhouses are still visible, and the elegant Homestead, at Hot Springs. To the southwest were little towns such as Stuarts Draft (where my friend's father was born), Middlebrook, Raphine, and Goshen, and the college-dominated town of Lexington, where my friends the Evanses lived. From Lexington I could cross the mountain on Route 60 and be in Amherst again.

In all directions, below the ridges, lay innumerable knolls and hills, pastures and cornfields of dense green, and the apple orchards for which the Shenandoah Valley is famous (there were cherries, too). The landscape was humanized by homesteads from the eighteenth century built by the Scotsmen who came down the Appalachians, farmsteads laid out by the German settlers and the white churches at which they worshipped, and antebellum houses of harmonious proportions with white columns, impressive façades, and lanes and lawns descending to the road. In addition to the panoramas available from Rockfish Gap and the drives along the Blue Ridge, there were topographical attractions, such as Natural Chimneys, Weyer's Cave and other caverns, Natural Bridge, and the Cowpasture, Calfpasture, and Bullpasture rivers, along with historical sites without number, from Jefferson's Monticello and Woodrow Wilson's birthplace (right in Staunton) to battle sites of the Civil War and the abandoned forges of Highland County.

My friend liked to drive; a trip across the mountain at Afton to Staunton was a matter of forty minutes or so, and he came often during the week and always on weekends, unless I joined him in Charlottesville or somewhere in between. Using county maps so that we could leave the main routes, we drove all over the state; and with historical guides and *Architecture in Virginia* in hand, we systematically visited scores of estates, houses, public buildings, and churches of the previous three centuries. Design was one of our major interests. I had never liked Victorian buildings and furnishings, but learned to appreciate the style in its best domestic examples—some with Italianate influence—and was also delighted to discover Federal architecture.

We visited or attended church at Saint Luke's (seventeenth century), Vauter's Church in Essex County, Bruton Parish Church in Williamsburg, St. John's in Richmond, the chapel of Washington and Lee University, and countless country churches where the Anglican service seemed to fit the setting and the architecture. We saw the interior as well as the grounds of the estates of the politically famous, from the Governor's Palace in Williamsburg and Madison's Montpelier to the Lee-Custis mansion. One wintry weekend, we visited Monroe's estate at Ash Lawn, in the company of my Aunt Margaret, such delightful company and so chic, despite her seventy-one years. Another December Saturday, we drove with a friend of mine, Jeannie, to Baltimore, where we ate crabcakes, and thence to Chincoteague and Assateague islands, on the Eastern Shore. The Atlantic treated us to a gale that blew cold rain and spray generously across the windshield and, when we stepped out of the car, our faces, but we still appreciated some of the characteristic buildings of the peninsula. The morning of our return, acquaintances invited us for a brunch, at which French 75s were served. Jeannie was a strong girl but not accustomed to alcohol: she became ill and on the drive via the Chesapeake Bay Bridge and Tunnel and back to Staunton—mostly in heavy snow—she lay moaning on the back seat.

We also went to White Sulphur Springs, Harper's Ferry, Baltimore, and other spots in surrounding states; and we drove a time or so to Philadelphia and New York, once coming back along the Eastern Shore of Delaware, and to Washington on several occasions, for dinners in ethnic restaurants, museum visits, music, and plays. At a performance of *Hello Dolly!* with Cab Calloway and Pearl Bailey, we saw Lyndon Johnson, the architect of the Great Society, climb onto the stage and join in the chorus, his arms around the stars and his voice booming out in his Texas drawl. There were few mishaps, though we often returned late, in crowded traffic along the well-traveled highways or by narrow winding roads. One Friday we rushed to Richmond to attend the opening of a major show at the museum, only to discover that we were mistaken about the date. I also took trips on my own, going to Washington to visit my cousin, an archivist, and to West Virginia, where some friends from Texas had moved. That trip, which could have been made quickly in the air, took me laboriously across one ridge after the other, climbing and descending ceaselessly, past hollows and through narrow gorges and then over still other ridges, with only country crossroad places to offer a bite to eat and some gasoline. On other weekends, I went to Lexington to stay with the Evanses.

At this remove, I do not quite see how there was time to do all this and yet teach and write. If there was a good poetry reading or a party in Charlottesville, or Martha Evans invited me to dinner in Lexington, I almost always said, "Why not?"—thirty-five or forty miles meant nothing. Now, except for major trips, infrequent shopping expeditions to a suburban mall, where I mingle with the Yats (the common folk of New Orleans and surrounding parishes), and an occasional social engagement that takes me across the city, I do not often leave Uptown New Orleans, doing most of my driving along St. Charles Avenue. I cannot believe it is only a question of age—or rather, one would have to ask how age in combination with other things has wrought changes. But certainly what I experienced then was the peculiar fullness of life associated with being young—mental and physical energies in abundance, the pursuit of parallel artistic and intellectual undertakings, and a coincidence of both with the enjoyment of splendid scenery and the fulfillment of love.

Byron makes his Childe Harold say:

> I live not in myself, but I become
> Portion of that around me; and to me
> High mountains are a feeling . . .
>
> .   .   .   .
>
> Are not the mountains, waves, and skies, a part
> Of me and of my soul, as I of them?

This explicit pathetic fallacy—the identification of the self with a landscape—on both the plane of the senses and that of the moral being or soul strikes us as foolishly romantic. Our contemporaries do not think of the environment, to which so much importance is assigned in the development of the individual, as being that of nature, but rather that of family, neighborhood, school, city, with, variously, their nurturing, their indifference, and their destructiveness; moreover, the implicit connection between feeling and soul might be considered empty, if not dangerous. But the fact is that the American landscape and the history that has taken place within it are highly romantic.

It is true that, in some ways, the land of Virginia and what has been built upon it struck me as classical. As the queen of the eighteenth-century colonies, it represents a sort of classic colonial style, illustrated in the restored buildings of Williamsburg. In architecture, the classical spirit is obvious: Jefferson, who introduced neoclassicism to the New World, used as his inspiration for the capitol in Richmond the Maison Carrée in Nîmes, France, and a drawing of the Pantheon in Rome as a model for the Rotunda at the university. Many other edifices in the state display the vigor of Greek Revival architecture (although it is romanticized). In the landscape, the harmonious contours of fields and hills and the soft colorations display—literally—what Gide called the classical "erosion of contours" and create harmony and moderation, suitable to human proportions—in opposition to the dramatic contrasts of Western landscapes, with their extremes of harsh light and shadow, their brutal snows and winds, their jagged peaks and deep gorges, their teasing distances. The political dream of eighteenth-century Virginia is, however, that of romanticism—the free man on his land, away from the corruption of court and city, living in harmony with a nature that man's mind allowed him to master but that still retained some of its original wildness, as a guarantee of goodness, just as the Blue Ridge, for all its pleasing lines and even coloration, is marked by rough stone outcroppings that bespeak the violent geological turmoils of earth's pristine epochs. And, though of classical lines, much of Virginia architecture even before the Victorian period shows romantic treatment.

To associate the land and its humanization with a single major esthetic, historical, and moral vision at the expense of the other is thus impossible. It is better to see them as a blend of different types of order—in dialogue with each other, nature, and man's needs and impulses. This dialogue is really that of human beings with themselves, the need for individualism in opposition to that for social order (if you wish, the struggle between liberalism and conservatism), the expansiveness of romanticism contrasting with the classical urge to delimit, summarize, stylize. These contrary impulses, following each other like waves, make up much of European and American cultural history. Gide defined classicism as a "tamed romanticism"; Valéry wrote that the essence of classicism was to "come afterwards." Even Wordsworth, that preeminent English Romantic, did not mean, when he spoke of the "spontaneous overflow of powerful feeling," that the feeling alone constituted the experience; it was, rather, the emotion as recollected in tranquillity (I like the *collected* part of that verb)—and formalized—that created the full esthetic experience of the poet, who was to communicate it to others rather than merely feed upon it himself.

Thus I can draw with confidence the parallel between setting and experience and say that the years I spent in Virginia, that cherry time of my life, were, on the personal plane, both romantic and classical. Romantic—for love, nature, and art collaborated to awaken fully my mind and senses in an expansion of feeling, to which Byron's ecstasy before the "high mountains" is not entirely foreign; classical—for the experience was an orderly one, ordered by a commitment to another, a sense of belonging, the belief in harmony and balance, and moral convictions that are now almost out of fashion but fitted so well into the context. As I drove eastward along Route 250 from Staunton, crossing fields and orchards and the South Fork of the Shenandoah River, then over Afton Mountain and down toward Charlottesville, winding past the noble properties of the previous century and neat fences demarcating the fields, it was always with a sense that my experience could be situated esthetically and morally with respect to some of America's noblest qualities and achievements of the mind and the eye—a relationship between the world and human efforts, in which the latter were realized harmoniously for both individual and collective good. Was it self-deception? To judge that would require more wisdom than I have. One has to hope (even the classicists would agree) that beauty of nature and of artifact, both written and architectural, mirrors or enhances some goodness in the heart: otherwise—unless one is merely a hedonist—why bother to search it out and cultivate it? Similarly, one has to believe that the blooming of one's youth has not been wasted, and that the time of cherries will precede an autumn of more fullness still, when the slow-ripening fruits of reflection, deliberation, devotion, and labor take on color, like the late apples of the valley and the leaves on Afton Mountain, gold, orange, and claret red, shining in the October sun.

On Men and Women

*A*s a girl, I spent many pleasurable hours of summer and after school with the neighborhood boys, playing softball in the street, climbing trees and building our clubhouse between two garages, making snow tunnels or inventing board games (we scorned the commercial ones) in my parents' basement on winter days, and, when I was older, cycling to the park and playing tennis. Now, decades later, many of my professional hours are spent in university settings among men, including meetings where I am the only woman—yes, even now—or one of few. In between, there were the years at Rice, where the men-women ratio was four to one, and, since then, the years of working with male colleagues and teaching male students, and, of course, time spent with male friends, lovers, husbands. Never have I felt uncomfortable around men, never have I considered them enemies. Strange creatures, yes; but not enemies. I even object—to pursue the military metaphor—to the notion of a war between the sexes.

Yet I have spent years poring over and teaching literature, especially by those connoisseurs of men and women, the French, much of whose writing is centered around just such a conflict. What does one find, it might be asked, from the fabliaux and farces of the Middle Ages, through Rabelais and Racine, then Stendhal, to Beauvoir's novels and the plays of Jean Anouilh—to take nearly random examples—if not a hostile confrontation between men and women, one which is taken as axiomatic, and which at best leads to an unsteady truce but more usually breaks out into overt aggression—at least verbal—and violence? In the medieval *Farce du cuvier,* the shrewish wife is abandoned in a vat; in Racine's tragedies, the sexes cannot, literally, live with each other and so must kill one another; Stendhal's novels are rich in metaphors of besieging, attacking, and conquering, although at best the sexual sparring can be resolved in genuine devotion.

Without the same violence and flamboyant endings, the French psychological novels of our own century, from Colette and Raymond Radiguet to Françoise Sagan, are just as centered on unending battles between men and women.

Surely. Among other functions, literature takes the ordinary dynamics of human relationships—sexual and conjugal, filial, social—and intensifies, concentrates, and sets them off to the point where the accidental, the conflicting, and especially the relieving are eliminated. Carried to their most dramatic extreme, the pure conflict and pure passion are singled out and lighted, so that human beings can see themselves both as they have the potentiality of being—for good and for ill—and, in the case of the ill, as they are saved from becoming, by countless circumstances and complexities of character and the grace of God. Perhaps Madame Bovary is all women; but all women are not Madame Bovary. That there is a thrill in living vicariously, without consequences, the high drama and high comedy of sexual confrontation cannot be denied. We return again and again to the sexual warfare in *Othello* and *Swann in Love;* such brilliant historical examples as Eleanor of Aquitaine and Henry II, and George Sand and Musset, are enhanced for our pleasure by literary treatment.

Yet I still do not like, as a characterization of relationships between the sexes, the generalizing term *battle,* at least in the realm of the quotidian, the lives most of us lead. My opposition to it is personal, practical, and philosophical, in the context of what now is and has been, not the utopian framework of what shall be (they claim) when, having won the putative war, the feminists have their day. (From what I have seen of Eleanor Smeal, Patricia Schroeder, Barbara Mikulski, and company, that utopia will truly be a vicious one. Far from carrying out their promise that, if given the opportunity, women will be more humane legislators and leaders than men, the female politicians who are now most in the public eye—drawing attention to themselves as politicians *for* women—are an aggressive and intolerant lot who would happily put their enemies in the stocks. I do not include in this number Peggy Wilson of New Orleans, an outstanding member of the city council; but, precisely, she is not considered by other women politicians as one of their own, an attitude demonstrated by the fact that when she ran for statewide office, no one added her name to the printed lists of females who might join the new administration.) Ann Richards, the current governor of Texas, is between the two types. She is concerned with putting women forward. This uncritical concern led her to appoint to the powerful Railroad Commission a patently unqualified Hispanic woman who, it turned out, is a liar also: although she claimed that she graduated Phi Beta Kappa from the University of Texas, it was revealed later that she did not graduate at all and was not elected to that illustrious society. Forced to acknowledge so, the woman appeared on television and wept. But Ann Richards is also a good-old-boy, a whiskey-voiced Texas politician of the old school, with all the charm and deceit that implies.

Here a digressive path beckons, into the thickets of relationships between those of the same sex. Those who are persuaded that men and women must, for the protection of the latter, consider themselves to be in generic enmity should find disconcerting the indisputably general phenomenon of rivalries and struggles of women among themselves (which are only camouflaged, not removed, by current appeals to sisterhood). Such rivalries, of which history offers dramatic examples, are explained away by aforesaid observers as an outgrowth of the false relationships into which *all* are thrown by the enmity between men and women—itself the fault of men, of course, since they, rather than what was once known as the fair sex, are the establishers and perpetuators of social structures. This explanation, it may be noted, does not take into account the biological parallels, at least among males: stags battle each other for a mate, not the mate. Perhaps this animal analogy is worthless; despite similarities, humankind is not identical in its needs, means, and scope to the beasts. Let us say merely that rivalries among members of the same sex are identifiable in the natural kingdom. My own sense is that, with exceptions (often sapphic in character), the positive dynamics between adult men and women are so strong that those enjoying them are wary of threats from the outside, and those left outside of them momentarily struggle to gain a place; the unwanted third is really at war with the duo.

What am I describing but a triangle? Even those who are not part of one are potentially so and look upon others as implicit rivals. If women dress for other women, it is not to *please* them, but to impose themselves as superior, that is, more desirable to a potential male observer. As for men, their barroom jousting and boasting is a performance for other men only in the immediate sense: mediated through others, whose attention acts to reassure them, it is directed ultimately toward the opposite sex, in its real or virtual representatives. Each member of a couple is ever on the alert for threats from an outsider of the same sex. Usually without intending it, I have found myself on various occasions the object of intense suspicion and dislike by wives whose husbands and I were acquainted professionally, or merely met at some social gathering. I think of an acid remark made (aside) years ago by the wife of my new department chairman when she first met me: "So this is what my husband brought back from Paris!" One man even reported to me—tactlessly—that his wife, alerted by subtle signs to his vague sentiment of admiration for me, had grilled him after our meeting to try to draw from him by the heat of her anger the reasons he found me attractive. The interrogation scene featured a hostile couple, but another woman was really the enemy.

What I will grant willingly (to return from my excursion onto the topic of backbiting women) is difference between the sexes— strangeness, I said before. The older we grow, the more we grow like ourselves, so that these differences are often more marked between older spouses than young ones. In all marriages countless ties are knotted by the years, it is true: the man and wife can finish each other's sentences, order dinner for one another, read the other's thoughts; they even come to look alike. But other ties weaken, notably the sexual drive that led them to each other and, if things went well, canceled or glossed over the friction between them, those irritants or *bosses* (bumps) that Gide portrayed so well in *The Counterfeiters*. No old man's or old woman's flaws will be refined or burnt away in the heat of passion or alambicated by the chemistry of bodies. So the differences become more visible. One has only to recall that, barely able to remember, barely able to communicate, Beckett's estranged couples are *old*.

Differences can be seen any day, however, at any age. When they have a collision on the freeway exits or get lost in a web of suburban streets, women cry; men get angry and curse. (Even the feminists admit this; a recent article by a feminist colleague refers us to research confirming the male reactions of anger and the female reactions of fear and supine body postures.) Women stop and ask directions when they need them; men, when lost, will drive on until dark or, as far as I can tell, indefinitely, unless they find their way by chance (which they will consider to be the result of reasoned calculation). Men spill sugar all around the side of the sugar bowl, and do not stop to think that the water they have just sloshed onto the table is running *under* the tray or placemat, not just around it. Women notice the football players' uniforms, men the plays. Women like to change the curtains, move the furniture, redo a color scheme; men leave things as they are—except for women, whom, without being asked, they will without a thought undertake to enlighten, that is, set right, on any subject whatsoever. Men ignore dirty fingernails, put luggage in the trunk upside down, are blind to ashes on a tie. A wonderful gentleman from North Carolina once put out his cigarette in a beautiful ornamental dish of polished wood I had put on a side table. Do I have to go on? I believe even that boys like trucks better than girls do, at a ratio of at least twenty to one, and are much more likely to throw sand in the nursery school yard. And, in this enumeration, I have not spoken even of such badges of the sexes as fishing trips—certainly the domain of the masculine—and the collecting of bric-a-brac and fabrication of useless objects, in which women excel. (In this connection, I shall note, woman though I am, my powerful dislike of handicrafts of any sort. This loathing I share with my husband, who, as a boy at camp in Tennessee, emulated Penelope by undoing each evening the beadwork he had been obliged to pursue during crafts hour, so that he would never finish the belt and thus at least would not have to proceed to another project. When we see televised scenes from geriatric establishments, we express the common hope that we will die before reaching such a place, because the inmates seem to spend the greater part of their hours making paper flowers and daubing finger paints.)

What is amazing, given the differences sketched above, is that men and women get along as well as they do. Sometimes it seems incredible that all marriages do not fall apart. Why, oh why, should I live (thinks the woman) with this slovenly creature who spills cigar ashes, wants the same meat-and-potatoes menus week after week, watches ball games until his head assumes the shape of a football, smells of beer, talks about tires and engines, doesn't get along with my sister, criticizes my mother, will not take me to the new restaurant that has just been reviewed in the paper, and grunts when I report the doings of my friends? How (asks the man) can I endure another week of this female, who owns twenty pairs of shoes, changes her mind several times a day, wants me to go visit her relatives, springs surprises on me, and talks while I am watching Notre Dame beat Pittsburgh? And these are among the most superficial, if most irritating, of differences. A whole complex of emotional and intellectual reactions of which each sex is barely aware characterizes its psychic continuum—ways of relating to parents, to children, to work, to acquaintances, to one's own sexuality; the understanding of leisure and the real and symbolic importance of money; ways of dealing with fear, grief, and failure.

But these are also the sources of human dynamics, without which we would be radically transformed and not for the better. Wasn't it a Frenchman who wrote "Vive la différence?" The sense of self, as Jacques Lacan emphasized through his investigations of what he called the mirror stage, depends upon the affirmation of identity in contradistinction to non-identity—the other. (Some nowadays are arguing for the child to be liberated from this other-directedness and grow up with only its own ego. A few such cases are already walking our streets, I fear.) Thought itself is a separation or tearing away of self-consciousness from all that it is not, namely, the world; such is, simply put, what Sartre meant by the nothingness of human reality. Since the very mechanisms of perception and reflection depend upon distinctions, monotony not only is boring but, at the extreme, obliterates all sense of what is. From time immemorial the imagination (in the fullest sense of the term) has turned around the contrasts between light and dark, day and night, sky and earth, water and air, summer and winter, not only meditating on them but using them as principles for understanding a range of other phenomena, from the same natural world to the self, the sexes (with their solar and lunar associations), and the domain of the metaphysical. The male-female polarity seems to go beyond itself and become attached to opposites such as thought and emotion. To know the other, personally and sexually, is to know richly through a distinction that intensifies self-recognition.

This indeed is the whole basis for attraction. Those who identify strongly with their sex enjoy their opposite. There are, to be sure, heterosexual men who do not quite fit the fishing-trip mold I alluded to earlier—men who fuss over their clothes, boast about their good Hollandaise sauce, talk lengthily about their migraine headaches, and like to visit their in-laws. This white-wine-and-quiche set is not my type. After all, *I* am a woman; I can make a sauce myself. (Anyhow, I loathe quiche.) What I want is the opposite, that male way of being, which may at times be vexing beyond words but has the charm of totalizing, with ease, all that I can never be except on the intellectual plane. This masculinity is, happily, available to me every day in the form of my cigar-smoking husband; it is also the impulse behind a great deal of literature—I think of Saint-John Perse's *Anabasis,* for instance. Doubtless this preference sheds some light on my choice to write repeatedly on the war novel, that male genre. It is also reflected in my tastes in American fiction: favorites include Dickey's *Deliverance* and Walter Van Tilburg Clark's *The Ox-bow Incident;* I liked even McMurtry's *Lonesome Dove,* although it is inferior to McMurtry's best work.

Lest it be supposed that I wish to valorize only the male principle—a position that today's feminists reproach Beauvoir, otherwise their *gurvy* (female guru), for adopting—I shall note at once my close friendships with a number of women—a cousin, college friends, students, colleagues—and my devotion to the mother, grandmother, and aunts who helped raise me. In addition, I observe with pleasure the joy so many men feel at seeing the feminine at work, in their lovers and wives—of whom I am one—and especially in their daughters. When that otherness, which they do not embody themselves and which they have courted and loved, is suddenly embodied before them in a young being who is, mysteriously, *of* them while yet being opposite—who often looks like them—well, there is usually no limit to their enchantment. The truly masculine man fears the feminine not at all, but rather enjoys it and can let it become part of himself. Valérie, one of only two named women characters in Malraux's *Man's Fate,* observes rightly that a woman is moved by nothing so much in a man as the union of tenderness and strength. Perhaps, it will be thought, she needs, Delilah-like, to find weakness in order to use it against his strength; rather, I would say, it reassures her that there is a place for her feminine qualities in his male realm. The French writer Roger Vailland fell forever from standing in my eyes when I read in one of his personal texts that he was always disgusted upon seeing a man carrying a child: for the true sense of strength is in its commitment to those who need it. Similarly, in all human beings, men *and* women, I look for vigor of mind, a trait long associated with the male of the species but which should be cultivated by all.

Identity, difference—we know, as Montaigne pointed out, only because the distinctions that I alluded to earlier, which are crucial in all epistemological thinking, are perceived within a context of similarities. Such is metaphor, which is the union of two dissimilars through a common feature. Fortunately, for human beings it takes very little of either difference or resemblance for psychological processes of distinction and identification to take place. Merely the fact of being recognized as an American by another American on a train in Italy is enough to create a bond of identity between two travelers, whose past and future may differ radically otherwise; merely the recognition that the person across from one is a member of the opposite sex suffices to reaffirm one's own sexual identity—and sometimes to establish a bond on the basis of reciprocal difference.

Why are professional women now so concerned about maintaining their onomastic identity? (It should be understood that I hope to offend no one by the following remarks—some of my friends are in the group referred to, and they may have good reasons for their choice.) A fortyish colleague of mine said, in the context of a paper supposedly on sixteenth-century social structures, that she found it deplorable that a woman should take her husband's name. But difference can be asserted within similarity; why not yield to the resemblance of name with the husband? In the first place, if they keep their maiden name, it still comes usually from a man—their father. We will probably encounter more of the matriarchal lineage in the professional class in the next decades, as it is already found in the housing projects of New Orleans; but lurking in the background *somewhere* for most women will be a paternal ancestor whose name they bear. The truth of the matter is that even the feminists can't get away from paternity. In the second place, there are practical difficulties to not sharing a spouse's name; we are all familiar with social awkwardnesses created thereby, and I do not think that dropping last names (as at a cocktail party: "Sara, this is Raymond"; "Hal, meet Elaine and Dan") is an adequate solution. What is to be done, moreover, about the children? Hyphenation is a solution. But it is easy to foresee, by the second generation, an awkward complex of four names (after Ms. Simpson-Goldstein marries Mr. Parks-Ward) that will make a Spanish grandee's string of patro- and matronymics look modest. Of course, maybe this hypothetical couple will not produce children. Ms. Simpson-Goldstein may have recourse to an abortionist. (In my view, such practitioners should be licensed and even subsidized through public or private insurance, but one would hope that to them only the most desperate would turn—those without mates, without funds, without prospects. At best, abortion is a very disturbing recourse. I recall hearing about a young woman who, after having had an abortion, said that when she saw photographs of a child growing in a maternal body, she knew that she had done something wrong.)

It seems to me that, in this age of militant feminist cultural criticism, perhaps it is time for a masculinist criticism. (The mostly phoney trend of "male bonding" via breast-beating and hot stones is not the sort of reaction I have in mind, though it may not be worthless, since presently it is the only one available.) I would scarcely be the one to launch such a body of thought, but it would be a pleasure to read that a publisher has just brought out a volume in which the brilliant new writer X decries the dominance of the current cultural scene by women, who are forcing their values onto him and thereby depriving him and, by extension, other males of their full sexual identity. For instance, the current view that it is good for men to weep—a view so widely accepted, since Edmund Muskie started the trend, that everyone from the retiring police chief to the coach who was just fired feels it incumbent upon him to shed tears at the microphone—should be combatted as profoundly undermining the nature of the male. The distortion of the language by such barbarisms as *s/he* and *his/her, chairperson* and *Cooperperson,* and, worst of all, *herstory* could be another target of such a critic's wrath, which, ideally, would lead to a call for legislation to prevent the largely ungendered English language from becoming rent by vulgarisms. (Lest the modifier "largely ungendered" be questioned, I shall point out, for instance, that perhaps only *mistress, hostess, waitress,* and *stewardess* remain familiar among feminine suffixes in -ess; moreover, they are now passing, the first replaced by "girlfriend" or some such euphemism, the second often unnecessary in today's casual social practice and largely confined to restaurant terminology, the last two replaced by "waiter" and "flight attendant." Even few animal feminines are current today. As for *man,* as my husband has pointed out elsewhere, it translates both *homo*—the species—and *vir*—the male.) Films such as *Mr. Mom* and *Thelma and Louise* would be attacked as subversive and viriphobic, perhaps even a violation of civil rights, since they single out one group for ridicule on the basis of that group's gender. If such a criticism prevailed, poems by Adrienne Rich, for example, would be tolerated in anthologies only with the warning that they are a product of bigotry.

I await the day when the Modern Language Association will have sessions devoted to such a masculinist criticism. Until then, let men beware: they are the objects, clearly, of a covert and not-

73

so-covert campaign to throttle and devalorize their characteristic ways of thinking and acting, bring their language under control, reduce their influence on the young, and lead them toward self-accusation, whereby they will finally recognize themselves as inferior and consent to domination by the other sex. Then, only a few women will be enlightened enough to believe that a man can be their equal in sensibility and sense, and deserves a place in the empyrean of the mind. God willing, I shall be one of them.

On Husbandry

It is eleven o'clock at night. My husband is lying on the bedclothes, in his pajamas; he is motionless. "What are you doing?" I ask. "I'm gathering strength to go brush my teeth." He manages to pull himself up and get to the bathroom, for that one indispensable act before bedtime. (Ten years ago a root canal operation, paid for dearly, convinced him of what no one had been able to persuade him until then: that he must take better care of his teeth. By that time his mother and father were past being able to say they had told him so.) He shuffles back, falls heavily onto the bed, and wearily reaches out to make sure his cigar butt, which probably hasn't been lighted for some while anyway, is extinguished. After a hard day of househusbandry, he is exhausted, yearning for rest.

This househusbandry, if you can call it that, was his idea. He had never found his teaching career to be very rewarding; fate had sent him to the wrong places, in difficult circumstances, and generally had given him students who were only faintly interested in learning any foreign language, and certainly would not pursue their linguistic studies far enough to provide him with classes in basic Indo-European linguistics, Sanskrit, comparative Greek and Latin grammar, Gothic—all the things he was educated to teach but which he rarely did, finding himself instead in French 101. What he really liked was research. He had spent everything he made and more (as well as much of his energy) on his first wife, an invalid for thirteen years, and had no personal wealth, but after his parents both died and their investments went to him, he decided that, frugal as he was, he could leave the university and become an independent scholar. We would divide the household expenses and the cost of raising our daughter and he would still have enough left over for bourbon and cigars. Staying home, seeing few or none for hours, following a narrowly circumscribed routine—such was exactly what he desired. To me he would leave the early morning rising, followed by the rush to the campus (after taking him his coffee in bed), then teaching, grading papers, conferring with students, ending the afternoon in the library or at a tedious, if not exasperating, meeting, then back home, facing dinner to prepare and an evening of work.

When we were first married, I discovered something that no one could have seen without living with the man: that, when he was at home (a home he now shared with me), he was a compulsive rocker—and a very good one, he claims. In a few months he had worn into my good blue rug two sets of deep grooves. Back and forth for hours—maybe reading, maybe just thinking, which he claims to do all the time and does not want mistaken for woolgathering. (He was delighted once to read the statement of a Nobel prize-winner in mathematics: that maybe thenceforth, when he sat staring at a clipboard, apparently doing nothing, his wife would believe he was really working.) Perhaps there *is* something to be said for the new morality, if living with a person before marriage would keep such surprises as mine from occurring. On the other hand would I have been willing to take up housekeeping with someone and wash his socks without benefit of a certificate that says, in the eyes of the law, that he is bound to support me (even if, strictly speaking, he does not) and our offspring? Probably not. And, had I known about the blue rug, would I then have declined to marry him? In that case we would have deprived our daughter of her life and the human race of her. Anticlerical though he was, Voltaire argued through his angel in *Zadig* that mortals should not have foreknowledge of the future; this probably applies to the institution of marriage. Paul maintains that his grandfather Lewis, who retired at age forty on modest reserves and then lived well into his eighties, owed his healthy longevity to his daily rocking (on his front porch if the weather was good) and to his frequent pails of beer from the corner bar in Indianapolis. Later I learned that the grandson started early, doubtless giving his parents, who had already deplored his tardiness in talking and his compulsive swinging, further reason to be concerned.

Retirement proved to be ideal for this activity, which may be, after all, merely his way of combining two essentials: exercise and rest—the latter more congenial to him perhaps because of his low blood-pressure (which may have been also what preserved Grandfather Lewis so long). The rocking chair—well over twenty years old, with its armrest now loosened—is in the den. Across the room is the door leading to the patio, to which he invites the dog to pass several times a day. The kitchen is immediately adjacent, with the refrigerator closest of all. That observation might be taken to suggest that he snacks frequently. Heavens, no. Nothing until lunch—no breakfast but coffee and orange juice—and then a modest midday repast, sometimes just cereal. The man has iron discipline when it comes to food and delights in shaming his wife and daughter, given to sweets and other morsels that help them keep up their strength. (Occasionally, however, he can take pride in my appetite: once at Campagno's restaurant he wanted to bet Tom Fromherz that I could eat more spaghetti than his wife could; the only reason the contest didn't take place, we believe, is that Fromherz was afraid he would lose.) In fact, I think Paul has in him a compulsion to deny himself things—like Uncle Earl, an uncle by his previous marriage, who, upon being told that his alcoholism would kill him, gave up liquor, then tobacco, then coffee and cola drinks, then ice cream and candy—except that Paul started with the candy and ice cream and hasn't yet reached tobacco and whiskey. No, the refrigerator's location is important because on its top are kept the dog biscuits, dispensed liberally throughout the day. In our household dogs are more privileged than people and never hear such cracks as "What are you eating now?" Another convenience is the proximity of the bathroom. Likewise close by is the coffee table with ashtray for the omnipresent cigar butt, a tray for coffee mug and pencil, and piles of books. At his side are the newspapers of the week, frequently held down by a suitably meditative cat.

Apart from letting the dog out and responding to what my grandmother referred to as the call of nature, his morning routine consists of reading the *Times-Picayune*. This is a very bad newspaper, getting worse by the year (not long ago gaudy colors appeared all over inside sections that had previously been immune to the horrible blue and red patches on the front page in imitation of *USA Today*). But it is the only paper New Orleans has. Paul has very high standards in his own writing—punctuation, spelling, and expression correct in every respect, in a thoroughly disciplined style with arguments like armor. So what does he see in the *Picayune*? Stories printed twice, others cut off in mid-exposition or with a section taken out in the middle, people referred to by last name without having been identified earlier, headlines stuck on the wrong article, "continued on page . . ." sections never found, misuse of words, atrocious spelling, and word-division done by a nitwit or a machine, or both. Each issue has at least one notice of apology for some inaccurate or mutilated article of the previous day. And I do not speak of the contents of the articles, those on politics and current events tolerably intelligent only if they come from the wire services and not always then, and the others being mostly celebrity journalism and cheap feature pieces of the sort you can find also in *People* magazine and *Psychology Today*. Some of the paper's writers have walked through the august Southern Gothic portals of Tulane University, but that seems not to have ensured that they write good prose. I have offered to subscribe to the New York *Times* for Paul; or he could buy it at Sidney's News, two blocks away. But there are two flaws in this plan: first, he is strongly Newyorkophobic; second, as he says, it is a much longer paper and he would never get anything else done.

The paper out of the way—sooner or later, according to the day of the week (Thursday's, with the food ads, seems to take a suspiciously long time)—he is ready for other activities. Here is where the husbandry comes in. A strange and interesting word, that. Webster's gives the first meaning, "care of a household," as obsolete, though perhaps, in today's two-career families with Mr. Mom, it should be revised. Its second meaning, "control or judicious use of resources," is known to students of English literature through Macbeth's observation, "There's husbandry in heaven." In that sense Paul excels at it. Except among those who cultivate fine speech, however, the word seems to have been used of late chiefly at western colleges of agriculture, or rather zooculture, that have programs in range animal husbandry or science, such as the University of Wyoming, which offers a Ph.D., and little Sul Ross State, where RAH majors, who give tone to the place, are known for both rodeo records and practical skills, including artificial insemination, with sheep, cattle, and horses.

Apart from what the courts of law call conjugal duty, my own husband's activities have not borne much resemblance to those of the RAH boys, and he neither talks nor dresses like them. But the cat and the dog—our domestic livestock—have to be fed and watered, and he does have other self-appointed household duties and supervision of resources (including his own, both financial and physiological). Some tasks require rising from the rocking chair, for instance making a pot of coffee or preparing frozen orange juice. He does the latter well, measuring the water with a meticulousness the producers probably did not foresee. Coffee is a little less routine. Having burnt out five or six electric coffee pots, we have fallen back on an old aluminum one you put on the stove. The problem is that it requires watching so it won't boil over—or it would require watching, except that he puts it on a very low flame so that it will never boil through the spout. The trouble is that this way it takes nearly an hour to perk; and even to reheat a half-pot takes twenty minutes, so if he wants coffee he has to think about it ahead of time and check on it once in a while, which is distracting.

Finally, after lunch, he's ready for an afternoon of research. Out come the Hittite dictionary, the *Vergleichendes Wörterbuch,* the Gothic chrestomathy (Gothic is the language in which he knows the Bible best), the piles of other dusty dark green or gray tomes with the spines half-torn. If it's a Tuesday or a Friday, he will interrupt his poring over the brittle pages to walk five blocks to the bank so he can deposit his checks, pay the cleaning woman on Tuesday, and buy our sandwiches and drinks at the Rendon Inn at the week's end. Then back to the books, or the yellow pad where he writes out in pencil his arguments concerning the Hittite words for domestic animals or how Old Germanic *w* became Old French *g.* (The great Charles de Gaulle was really plain old Karl of the Wall.)

One of the principal research undertakings of my husband in

the last ten years has been a study of the Indo-European gender system. As his series of a dozen or so articles proves, the masculine and neuter arose before the feminine; the latter is a third gender, an historical afterthought. Now this clearly has political implications for the present—or it can, if one insists upon "reading" language in gender terms. If he were to try to draw anthropological and social conclusions, rather than just linguistic ones, he might conclude that this development indicates the inferiority of women. For, househusband though he be, he is also a thoroughgoing *phallocrate,* as the French call the male chauvinists. He agrees with the apostle whose name he bears: "Wives, be subject to your husbands." He claims not to believe at all in equality of the sexes, nor in equal privileges. Womenfolk are supposed to do the laundry, the cooking and washing up, the childcare, gardening, marketing, and cleaning; working women, like me, can be allowed domestic help, but let them not ask their husbands to do laundry or cook. In his family—for his father and himself—women have even served as chauffeurs. His chief personal exceptions to this principle are taking out the garbage—because he likes to organize it in the trash cans according to mysterious systems of classification and rotation—and helping plan the menus for the week, lest I decide on a Southwestern abomination such as enchiladas.

You might think that resentment would have grown in me like Spanish moss choking an oak. But my views on this topic are a strange hybrid. I have thought about the feminine condition ever since I was five or so and had to put on a dress for special occasions, although I wanted to stay in jeans, the outward and visible sign of my inward and spiritual self-identity. None of my playmates put on dresses, for the good reason that they were all boys. When, a little later, my mother forbade me to appear at the screen door in pajamas when John Hall from next door came around early in the morning, I discovered that the vestimentary code had not only social implications but others that I subsequently identified as sexual. This and fifty years of additional experiences in the world of men, and women, make me as good an authority on the feminist issue as Gloria Steinem. A *phallocrate* I obviously cannot be, but perhaps I am something of the equivalent, in what some perceive as the gender war, of Uncle Tom. Of all the differences that separate me from today's radical feminists, perhaps the crucial one is the simple fact that I have liked, and loved, men too much to want to deprive them of some of the very qualities that make up their charm: their intense physical presence, their peculiar habits, their authority, if you will. What successes I have had with them are inseparable from my image of their assertive manner, and for the failures I blame neither their masculine ways nor my own feminine ones. Starting with John Hall, my father, and my grandfather, I looked upon them as both fellows in the egalitarian world of mind and interests—to which I had entire access from childhood—and beings whose difference was desirable and, in some sense, superior. One accepted their decrees, tried to please them—ah yes!—and, as I learned at a later age, desired them. Knowing this, a Freudian-minded reader will need nothing more: the whole complex is visible, isn't it? But I will make their case even easier: my father's name was Paul, and my husband's name is Paul, and that is not the only similarity between them.

Having said this much, I shall add that I do not care a fig for Dr. Freud, who may have liberated some but whose influence has generally been pernicious, nor for his intellectual offspring, including those academicians who have turned literary criticism into the uncovering of mental illness. It seems to me that nowadays more people believe in Freud (and Paul de Man, the late deconstructionist guru) than in God, but I don't see how such belief has advanced their lives in any way, and more often than not it leads them to a couch from which they arise as broken as before—and separated from a sizeable sum of their money. Besides, it is not explanations, scientific or otherwise, that I am interested in, but values and especially those that lead to meaningful action, which includes art. In Nietzsche's words, man is not a problem but a solution. So what if one has a complex? Less important than the scar on the personality, if such it be, is what one can make of it—as Malraux put it, the scar one leaves on the world. Let the Freudians hang themselves with analysis while I return to the topic of feminism.

In truth, I like my husband's old-fashioned supposition that his wife will wait on him and do his bidding. It is reassuring. I used to hear quoted at home a phrase from some English novel: "My father made a sign, and my mother left the room." I am quite willing to leave the room, so to speak, and find it perfectly natural that his desires should come first. *First,* I said—not *only.* These desires obviously include some oddities. That I should work while he stays home is odd by both the old system, according to which it should be the reverse, and the new, which demands shared labors. Unlike the typical American male, however, he does not identify himself with his job. Not working—except on the occupations of the mind—he resembles his contemporaries less than the eighteenth-century squire he should have been born, who would have thought it perfectly fitting simply to survey his estate for a few hours on a summer morning and then busy himself with his books.

I, on the other hand, like activity, which can create meaning if properly channeled. "Man reveals himself by undertakings," wrote Sartre. More precisely, despite the failings of the university, I like my life there. Doing laundry and wheeling the cart through the supermarket aisles are *not* immediately very significant, granted. But we do want to eat, after all—even Paul—and have clean clothes. My mother and grandmother did these chores; am I to set myself up as better than they?

"They also serve who only stand [sit?] and wait." The human economy does not resemble the divine one very much, but we can at least allow this. If sacrifice there be, it is a very small one for having a contented husband in his rocking chair. There are worse tasks than doing dishes. And what human being, man or woman, has not had to suffer tedium, exchange one advantage for another, put up with the uncomfortable? Georges Bernanos pointed out that in this life everyone serves in some sense: better to serve another, or something one believes in such as family or cause or country, than to serve one's own selfish impulses for sixty years. If you don't believe it, look at the face of a superannuated playboy or a rubicund old politician who has gotten fat on graft. Besides, do my friends see me suffering? I have written what I wanted, taught what I wanted, and, on some occasions, Paul has eaten soup and hot dogs for days on end so that I could go back West or to France in the summer. Nor should this suggest that he is a browbeaten male who, despite appearances, has lost his authority to a woman. Being a gentleman, he knows full well that such is only fair play. If truth be told, he really likes only intellectual women anyway.

But I said my views on the feminist matter were mixed. This is because this willingness on my part to assume the wifely domestic role is accompanied by a strong vein of feminism, of my own brand, which antedates that of NOW and Gloria Steinem and Betty Friedan, not to mention the radical lesbians. Far from doing my late-day domestic chores out of a spirit of true deference while the househusband rocks away the cocktail hour with a bourbon-and-soda, I do them with a bemused irony and a slight sense of superiority—not superior to him, for he has his own kind of excellence, but to those of more limited scope, since I see us as having both accepted *and* adapted the traditional functions of the sexes. This is hardly the attitude for Auntie Tom. Or is it? Perhaps it was shared by our great-grandmothers. Was it my pioneer ancestors on my mother's side, who crossed the Great Plains under conditions we can scarcely imagine, or my paternal grandmother, a graduate of Mount Holyoke College, who, given a few months to live by the doctors in Montreal, went out West, married, had six children, traveled over much of the world, and lived until age eighty-eight? Anyway, someone certainly gave me the idea that women could do almost anything—provided, of course, they didn't appear at the door in pajamas—and at no time of my life would the idea have crossed my mind that I couldn't do mathematics, or travel, because of my sex.

Mind you, I would not have attempted to go where I was not wanted—men should have the prerogative of a smoking room, a club, a locker room to themselves. Attempting to integrate a male institution would not have occurred to me; the racial issue and the sexual one are entirely different. But, contrary to what is sometimes supposed about the fifties, the civilized world then offered to women nearly every profession except military combat units. (On that score I will say simply that I would rather be defended by any man, especially a young muscular one, than by myself, weighing in at one hundred pounds.) Rather than seeking separate curricula—what are now called Women's Studies and strike me as regressive—many of us assumed that our educational right was to study, if we chose, what men studied—a nongendered intellectual patrimony of arts, letters, and science. My apartment-mate at the old Rice Institute was the first woman ever to be graduated there with a mechanical engineering degree—not that it hadn't been allowed, but simply because women generally aren't interested in mechanical engineering, any more than little girls like trucks. Thanks to my literal-mindedness, for much of my time there I ate dinner in the men's dining hall, the lone female in the place simply because, as I explained before, there being no such hall for women, it was open to out-of-town girls also, and it made sense to go there, even if the others, too self-conscious, refused.

More fortunate than most, I have the sense to recognize that to be able to do it all is a privilege granted to few, those few often being of the fair sex. This attitude is not for all, granted. Nor is that of NOW, although the constant publicity it receives makes people take it as gospel instead of merely one position among many. Wife abuse, both physical and mental, is a real evil of our society, and those who suffer from it may even need the attentions of some of the doctors I maligned earlier. But being a woman has its own kind of hubris, which should serve not to separate us from the men but to make each sex understand the other. Pride is a common tongue. This brings me back to the linguistic question. Far from agreeing with such radicals as Monique Wittig and Sande Zeig, two feminists who, in an effort to recover a language that they consider stolen from women by the males, have composed a lesbian dictionary to replace the standard one, I consider language to be a particularly rich and privileged commonality. While it can be misused, as in fascist and racist rhetoric, it is still the broadest and most sensitive ground for understanding. So what if English, unlike Greek and Latin, uses the same word to indicate both the male of the species and the species in general? I have long thought that all great writers, and many lesser ones, have been in some sense androgynous, uniting in themselves the male and female ways of seeing the world. Perhaps some of the best marriages, and the best husbanding of human resources, come from the ability to make of one's sexual situation the context, but never the entire text, of the self.

On Language—and Teaching It

$\mathcal{M}$y calculus and analytical geometry professor at Rice, a refugee from Vienna who came by way of the Institute for Advanced Studies in Princeton, could not pronounce English well. Once, when returning to me a test that bore a "2" (the Rice equivalent of a B), he announced, "Vell, Miss Hill, no vun." But Herr Reiter was an excellent teacher, with a good classroom manner, and was personally interested in his students' progress. He sometimes discoursed on the beauty of mathematics, which, he pointed out, was both the queen and the handmaiden of the sciences.

So it is, I think, with languages, not a branch of science, to be sure, but—as linguistics has shown—not entirely unlike it (after all, Indo-European tongues evolved according to demonstrable principles of phonology and morphology, and even loose-boned English has something of the system about it). Language is the servant, certainly, of all the other bodies of knowledge (even mathematical formulae, printed with only figures, have verbal equivalents); it is the instrument and enabler of our very thought processes. "The limits of my language are the limits of my world," wrote Wittgenstein. Some would add that language is at the center of our being, the principle of creation. "In the beginning was the Word." Like mathematics, though, language is also the enabler of itself, its own *raison d'être,* whose illustration goes beyond itself to point to something else, which we call *world,* and which can yet be without any justification other than itself and its own creative powers.

To teach language, then, is to offer at once a means and an end. Even in the form of a barely half-mastered foreign tongue, language has the power to multiply the students' knowledge and experience as few other instruments can do. Perhaps, moreover, no other academic discipline ranges so from the objective to the subjective; only philosophy would come close. Thus language is kin and congenial to, and useful to, both those who deal with facts alone and those who deal with the most radical assertions of subjectivity—what Kierkegaard described as "an objective uncertainty held fast in an appropriation-process of the most passionate inwardness." Like the scientist, I am able to say with respect to such matters as spelling, agreement of adjectives and past participles, use of pronouns, and sequence of tenses (I choose these examples almost at random), "Right or wrong; there are no gray areas." I urge my students to consider the language as something to be used rigorously; their challenge is to learn it well enough to make it as exact, as revealing as possible. Along with mathematicians, scientists, and some philosophers, I can thus encourage systematic thinking and help wage war against those whose understanding of higher education is that it is a matter of expressing one's opinion (informed or otherwise). (This personal campaign is reminiscent of a view of the old schoolmasters, who held that the study of Latin would improve students' thinking. The modern language has replaced the ancient one, but the claim is the same.)

At the same time, to more advanced students, who, by learning their grammar rules and vocabulary, have earned the privilege to read and write subjectively, I can present, for their edification and critical considerations, a selection of literary material whose meaning is, if not entirely arbitrary, directionless, unidentifiable or nonexistent (I do not subscribe to deconstructionism), still a matter of uncertainty and subjectivity, or at least variations in emphasis, because of the inherent ambiguities of language, authorial effort to cultivate them or inability to resolve them, and, chiefly, the human contents—matters of value, emotion, and behavior. In particular, like the poet Valéry, I recognize, and can show students, that the areas where rigor is superseded by inexplicable harmonics of sound and meaning are often the most compelling as well as the most beautiful uses of language.

In short, I have spent much of my career drilling students in elementary French and advanced French grammar—a course I enjoy teaching and am sometimes fortunate enough to have students enjoy with me—while in the same term presenting the prose and poetry of such as Proust, Gide, Sartre, Camus, Baudelaire, Claudel, Valéry, and Apollinaire—that is, inviting students to find significance and value, ranging from the esthetic to the moral and metaphysical, in these marvelous fabrications of the French tongue. Of course such instruction is really a matter of the students' educating themselves, since, beyond the acquisition of some basic information the professor can provide about authors, periods, and works (I do not scorn it), the study of literature is an experiential one. If, as Barthes wrote, "the gift of language is the gift of the self," this is true for the author, who offers himself in the text; the teacher, who serves as intermediary between the text and the novice reader; and finally the reader, who, through another's language, comes to know additionally or differently, and thus to discover another side of the self.

Determined from some time in my adolescence to write, I knew that I would not make my living that way only; lyric poets cannot produce verse forty hours a week, and such immense quantities of poetry would not sell anyway. Of course I could have considered what can be called the garret life—living without means, more or less. Ruling it out was not a question of snobbery. Living modestly is more appealing to me than living in an extravagant fashion, and inconveniences such as lack of hot water or shabby surroundings would not have kept me from living in a walk-up flat in New York, had that been my choice; when I came to New Orleans I purposely settled in a lower-middle-class neighborhood. But, for one thing, at no time did I want to settle in the literary colonies of New York or San Francisco, to which some acquaintances repaired in their early twenties. (Paris would have been another matter. As I told friends years ago, Paris had everything— not every*one*—I needed. But what it would have required for me to live there I was not ready to allow.) For another, the idea of living on expedients is intolerable to me; it is counter to my need for regularity and also poses a vague moral threat. In any case, that is not a full life. Journalism did not interest me, and patronage is out, in our time. And I wanted to pursue the intellectual life—since literature as I see it is not entertainment chiefly but the pursuit of truth. So college teaching it would be.

In any case, I came to the business early and honestly. At a young age, I mimicked my teachers at home, arranged my books like those in the school library, wrote "readers," and, through classes on the front steps, tried to impart knowledge to those neighborhood children younger than myself. Some well-trained and devoted teachers—hard disciplinarians, perhaps, but fully engaged in the process of shaping minds—set excellent examples for me; among them were a number of instructors in history, science, and language, including Professors Drew, McKillop, Mansfield, and Bourgeois, all so important to me. In my family, there were teachers on both sides. My grandfather Hill taught chemistry in addition to practicing medicine, and my grandfather Stanforth taught for some years, although his last position was with the Gates Rubber Company. Perhaps I should mention also my great-uncle Commodore Stanforth, a Methodist minister. What teacher of literature does not have something of the moralist? My aunt Mary taught, variously, Latin, English, history, and biology in various Colorado schools while also giving piano lessons. My cousin Frances was in charge of a one-room schoolhouse in Tarryall; my father found teaching the calling to which he was most suited.

As for my mother—well, she was born to it, the most natural teacher of all these family members. Determined to pursue a career in the classroom, she put herself through Colorado Teachers' College in Greeley, taught, as I have said before, in small towns in Colorado and Wyoming, went to the University of Chicago for a master's degree in social psychology, and returned to Grant Junior High School in Denver, where she met my father, her student teacher. In Wyoming, she tutored the feebleminded daughter of a prosperous ranch family so successfully that the woman learned the mechanics of written English—I swear—as well as most of my students (good spelling, no comma splices); her chief compositional flaws, as shown in letters, were that she expressed the reactions of a ten-year-old child and repeated herself because she had no memory of what she had already written. At the end of her life, my mother was still tutoring—pupils with dyslexia, or Mexican children who needed assistance with English, or sons of prominent families who expressed their rebellion against their social world by refusing to do well in school.

I do not claim to have my mother's talent, nor to have exercised my efforts with the humble and neglected, as she often did, nor to have had her success, which came in part from her commitment to each child. It was partly also a question of patience; perhaps mine has gone into other things, and perhaps I have needed to assert its limits. The differences in our careers involve also the level of instruction, both quantitatively and qualitatively distinct, as well as the whole institutional and social context in which I have pursued this calling. Teaching at a private institution of higher learning has led me to hold two convictions in particular. The first is that, given the handsome price charged to our students, the faculty is morally obligated to provide not only quality classroom instruction but also professorial guidance—called "personal attention," or sometimes "interaction"—beyond the classroom. Surely I would not claim that this obligation has always been met on campuses of private institutions with which I am familiar; there are indolent and incapable professors, with old yellowed notes and droning voices, who teach nothing beyond the rote mechanics of a subject, and there are those—sometimes the same—who are rarely available for student conferences and might have little to offer anyway. But to me, classroom preparations and office conferences are both a serious business; in this respect, I follow the maternal example. The second conviction is that, students having chosen to come to this university, *they* are obligated to follow our rules and meet our standards. This is sometimes called the "implied contract." It simply makes sense that they should receive the value we provide according to the ways in which it is officially determined. (If it did not take me too far from my topic, I would go even farther and argue that they have an obligation also to themselves and to society; after all, *someone*—parents, trust fund, scholarship—is paying for their education at a premium rate, with moneys that represent the fruit of labor and the resources of the nation.)

Hence, if students in a required language course, for instance, kick against the pricks and perform on a level commensurate with their bad attitude (and then complain, too), I have little patience for them. "What!" they might say—for example, the student who skips the class before Thanksgiving and then comes to my office hour the next week to find out "what was covered in class"— "You are supposed to be available to help students; that's why I came to a place such as Tulane, instead of . . . [pick any—LSU or SUNY or Ohio State]." Yes; but—for one thing—the university is paying me—*you* are paying me—to use my time judiciously and profitably according to my understanding of my responsibilities, an understanding that does *not* include repeating material for someone who skipped it; and, furthermore, to encourage such bad habits is not helping anyone. Moreover, the real reason the student came here is that Edward Fiske's *Selective Guide to Colleges* ranks Tulane very high on the social scale, noting that New Orleans is itself a party. (The *Princeton Guide* has recently followed suit by proclaiming Tulane one of the leading party schools. As often, appearances *are* reality.) So my attitude is somewhat hard-nosed. It does not rule out, however—at least I hope not—a generous-minded gesture now and then to my students and the moral persuasion that I owe them a great deal, by virtue more of being who I am than what I am—that is, for moral, not professional, reasons.

As the aphorism about Mark Hopkins and the student on the log suggests, the best teaching usually is a matter of minds, perhaps just two minds, in close contact. Small classes, which I am fortunate to have usually, allow for such confrontations, in which the verbal exploration of texts and ideas by several people working at once expands understanding. Compositions and research papers, if shaped and evaluated properly through professorial guidance, are another type of confrontation: detailed comments on an essay or draft, followed by a conference with the student, rewriting or new writing, and more comments. After a semester or so of this, what student style would not be developed? Teaching writing should not, however, be a matter of indoctrination; English instructors are wont to overstep the bounds greatly and frequently in this respect. The phenomenon is not just a recent one. At Rice, an English instructor told an acquaintance of mine that he was going to rearrange her mental furniture. That she ought to be exposed to other intellectual styles is quite appropriate; that her own mind should be redesigned by the instructor's fiat is less so. If it is *inevitable* that professorial views should enter into classroom presentations and evaluations of writing, indeed into the very choice of material, there is no reason for such views to be imposed deliberately.

My approach to teaching thinking is less dogmatic than that of many, and more (I dare imagine) like that of Montaigne and another of my literary models, Gide, whose didactic interest (a leading current in his thought) was in eliciting self-awareness in his readers but not in imposing a single standard or view. Again, language is the primary tool for such awareness. Even in a lecture-cum-recitation class such as Advanced Grammar, it is possible to teach a bit of systematic and critical thinking, using just the materials at hand—the language and its semantic and grammatical elements, not my own opinions. Boileau's esthetic principle that what is well conceived will be clearly enunciated has as its converse the principle that lucid enunciation contributes to examination and clarification of thought. Moreover, if one wishes to educate in the sense of "leading out," that also is favored by the personal bond—the *language* bond—which enhances development of the mind and the moral and esthetic sense. I often feel what H. R. Swardson calls the true pleasures of teaching: first, the pleasure of helping, next, the "axiological pleasure"—"pleasure in inspiring students, instilling values in them."

The students sense this, I am convinced. Why otherwise would a few similarly minded friends and I who teach French end up by writing twenty or thirty recommendations a year for students applying to graduate schools and professional schools, or seeking employment? This is true for me even though, as one of the very few traditionalists left at the university, I call students by their last names. (That way, we are on an even footing with respect to social niceties. And I can always become more informal later, if that seems appropriate, whereas I can maintain properly formal terms with those students for whom the academic reports may not be good.) The first week or so, members of my classes feel uncomfortable at being so addressed, supposing their professor to be cold, aloof, arrogant; by the third or fourth week, they know otherwise, realizing that their name represents to me a full person, whose aspirations are taken seriously even if mistakes in French get the red pen. By the end of the term, they know that they will not be forgotten and can return to my office any semester for recommendations, or for assistance with French, or to offer or receive candid judgments on matters intellectual, social, and moral. They realize also that, although the class contrasts with more leisurely and open-ended courses, the methodical way of proceeding, the emphasis on meeting standards, the express-train speed, with only brief stops, have led them to a higher ground of knowledge, not only of grammar but of their minds and themselves.

With all this praise of language and its possibilities, it may appear unseemly for me to say, at this juncture, that I am grateful to that chance or providential intervention that led me to make my career as a teacher and critic of a *foreign* tongue and literature, not my own. For do they not similarly illustrate the same power and beauty? Surely. I should not care to venture a judgment on the respective value, potentiality, or semantic or phonetic beauty of English and French, despite the greater lexical richness of the former and its peculiar appeal by virtue of having, for so many actions, objects, and concepts, *two* words, the one from Germanic, the other from Latin through Middle French. And, since my father ended his career by lecturing on American literature, how can I suggest that such a calling is not at least as attractive as my own? Moreover, it almost goes without saying that some of my best friends are professors of English. But foreign language appealed to me from my earliest encounters with Spanish, as a girl. Perhaps I simply like challenges; why not learn to write in the *foreign* language, to double one's capacity of expression, and why not then teach it to others with the same aspiration? There is also the serendipitous increased awareness of one's own tongue, an advantage observed by students even at the undergraduate level and commented on by authors such as Ionesco and Beckett. Perhaps also I am attracted by the otherness that the foreign tongue constitutes, almost as fully as does another human being. But these observations merely indicate the pleasures of French for me, not my particular reasons for rejoicing at not being in an English department.

Those who know English departments may need no further explanation. But for those who see such institutions only at a distance, a bit of elaboration is necessary. In a large university, English is a populous organization, serving as it does all, or almost all, students at least once and having large numbers of majors— many empty-headed—and, often, numerous graduate students, whose chief concern is getting their own careers started. Some of the worst, as well as the best, of teachers gather there. If my observations are accurate, in the area where the teaching of writing should be of the greatest concern—in some classes, the *only*—it is often disregarded. The students are sometimes treated very shabbily by their graduate-student instructors; papers receive grades without being read, syllabuses are cast aside in favor of a loose class organization featuring discussions that require no preparation, and writing assignments are eliminated to reduce the time required for grading. At the other end of the spectrum are the full professors, who characteristically do not deal with freshmen and who may teach as few as three or six hours per semester. In between are the teachers of composition and rhetoric, occupying the status of drones.

Moreover, for two or three decades now faculty in English have been divided, usually officially, into "critical" and "creative" experts. As the writer-in-residence, the poet or novelist is separated from the teaching of those masterpieces whose qualities would instill in their readers some of the understanding and sensitivity that would make them better writers also. (Perhaps this statement should be qualified somewhat. A recent piece by Garrett in the *Sewanee Review* points out that since "theory" has arrogantly taken over many English departments that used to be devoted to teaching literary history and criticism and what is now attacked as "the canon," creative writing programs are, on some campuses, the only locus for what Monroe Spears calls "old-fashioned humane teaching of literature." So things are even worse than I first suggested.) From the writer's point of view, furthermore—

though this is a different matter—the position of chaired poet or novelist is often inimical to the creative life. Worst of all, a spirit of cronyism has come to prevail among those who teach writing in the universities such that the whole matter of writing, publishing, and giving readings has become almost incestuous. Being on the other side of the hall, so to speak, I have taught masterpieces and, indirectly, good writing through them, but have not been labeled either "critic" or "creator" and have remained distant from the narrow world of, alternately, back-biting and back-scratching circuit poets.

So much for English departments. I was speaking about teaching, the sort that uses objective material to enrich a student's subjective life. That vast sums are necessary to support the kind of teaching I have in mind is undisputable. It requires a trained human being and his time—and human time is nearly the most expensive resource we have. (The appropriate remuneration for such trained human time is a matter of dispute. "Much too low," say most of those affected; and they have succeeded in persuading the public at large that professors are very ill-paid—some decades after this is no longer true. To support their contention, they point to corporate lawyers, executives, or perhaps just the clerk of court of Orleans Parish . . . "Too high," say a few timid voices, who dare not speak louder for fear of being set upon by the others; "let those who claim that their services are so valuable get positions in government, business, or industry to prove it . . . ") In some disciplines, or subfields thereof, such as literary studies in French, education requires also a vast investment in a library that must be constantly renewed and expanded. In other disciplines such needs are even greater, and I am wholly sympathetic to the scientists, from the nuclear physicist to the mycologist, who require, for teaching as well as research, elaborate equipment and supplies, in large laboratories, for which the budget dwarfs our little expenditures for paper and printing ribbons. Yet I do not subscribe to the view that money, and money alone, will produce excellence. With respect to capital investment, physical facilities for the sort of teaching in which I am engaged can be simple: a pleasant and private office, accessible to students, a classroom with good lighting and blackboards, and typing facilities for the many drafts. Often, all that is required is a professor, a few students, good books, and time for discussion—*not* elaborate realia and princely surroundings.

Yet, whatever the material requirements, higher education is an expensive undertaking, whether the university pays a full professor to teach two or three classes of fifteen or twenty students each, or a chemist to lecture to two hundred but also carry out and supervise research in a million-dollar laboratory. How, it may be asked, can society afford it; or how can affording it be justified? There is an economic answer to such questions, namely, the commonplace that in today's technological and commercial world society *must* afford sophisticated training for its members, on pain of failing otherwise in its industrial and political challenges.

But such an answer, however true it may be, interests me little. Rather, I should prefer to look at the matter from a human, almost an existential, angle. What can be more important to human beings than their own development? "Man is the end of man," said Marx. Consider the investment of society in such matters as social events—weddings, baptisms, proms, balls, country club dances, Christmas parties, the ceremonials of death—and weigh it against the commitment to train minds, or, if one prefers to confine the matter to concrete terms, merely to teach a little history and political science, a bit of philosophy and physics to those who will direct the businesses and cities of the next decade. Think also of the lengths to which, as a society, we go in order to prolong life by medical treatment and devices. It may be observed, of course, that weddings, parties, and funerals—not to mention health care— create jobs; but such is true also for the university. The trouble that civilized human beings take to sustain, adorn, transform, or channel their physical persons and energies—the eating and drinking they must do to preserve their existence, the cultivation of their sexuality and of their tendencies toward activity and natural aggressivity, their obligation to die—should not be greater than their efforts to transform their minds by developing raw potential into rational thought, knowledge, and creativity. An immanentist would observe that this is perhaps what Christ meant by saying

He had come that we might have life, and have it more abundantly. The human project—by that I mean the physical and metaphysical impulse toward self-preservation, self-realization, and self-expression—so often assumes forms that are socially unacceptable and thus it presents a moral dilemma: allow the behavior and put society at risk, or eliminate the behavior and stifle the impulses that make the individual what he is. Thank heaven that there is a form known as education that, even if expensive, is at least not clearly harmful and, at worst, is an expensive luxury. Nor do I think merely that sending students to the university will keep them off the streets for a few more years.

Now there is a danger in teaching, and the more attractive the teacher finds his role, the greater the danger. What I am referring to is power. "Knowledge is power," said the Greeks. If that is true, it is the students who, properly, are being empowered by professorial efforts, toward ends for which they alone will be responsible, after our collective efforts to shape them are concluded. But, by means of this language, *my* knowledge also gives *me* power over other human beings. As an heir to a long tradition, both political and religious, that sees power as dangerous, I find this disturbing. (While Rousseau's Protestant and enlightened insistence upon self-governance—that is, the role of both conscience for the individual and popular sovereignty for the state—is congenial to me, he nevertheless puts me off, because he is not wary enough of collective power. Voltaire's ranting against the church— "l'infâme"—shows sounder instincts.) Yet I subscribe to the Socratic idea that all men choose for themselves what they deem to be the good: hence this power must not be too distressing to me. Although numerous students of mine over the years have railed against the short-answer questions on their test papers and the mathematical formulae for assigning grades, I do not really think that we who follow such procedures are the new fascists. Indeed, common sense tells me that, since distinctions *must* be made if any sort of competence—technical and intellectual—is to be maintained in this country, it is well that these distinctions be made by those who are experienced in the matter and have, at least publicly, committed themselves to as much impartiality as they can muster.

Age and training do not guarantee responsibility and wisdom, but throwing grading out the window—or papers down the stairs, the lowest getting an F—or having students grade one another, as an English instructor did here once, is less certain to produce equitable assessments than if one follows an old-fashioned method of assigning points on the basis of objective or at least somewhat standard criteria.

So much for the question of evaluation and professorial responsibility. Morally and socially significant, no doubt, this responsibility is still less obvious than that of all manner of governmental employees, attorneys, doctors, engineers, diplomats, agriculturists, and so forth, in whose hands and minds our individual and collective welfare rests day after day. That we teachers of language and literature nevertheless are engaged at more than a living wage, usually for a lifetime, to spend a few hours of our time per week in the classroom, a half-dozen or so on committees and administrative matters, another half-dozen on grading, and the rest *reading* is quite amazing. While there may be considerable time spent on such often-tedious tasks as preparing and grading tests, reading student essays, and seeing to other routine matters, in the course of an academic year (not to mention the summer) there are many hours available for pursuit of research, and this research is a matter of my choosing, not another's. In my case, it may even include writing such as that I am doing now. I am thus paid to do what I would gladly do otherwise, pursue the life of the mind. What great good fortune to have a personal vocation correspond with a livelihood. No matter that the combination leads to my spending all evenings save Friday, long hours of the weekends, and most of the summer at tasks that outsiders scarcely know exist, and that would seem to them now onerous, now ridiculous; the whole life of the scholar-writer should be, by its very nature, one of commitment, with a minimum of contingency and a maximum of choice. What better definition is there of freedom?

The Feminist in the Cupboard

$\mathcal{M}$y aunt Margaret Stanforth, as a young woman, knew she would have to support herself and probably assist her aging parents, who were not well. Unlike my mother, she was not drawn to the university, with its opportunity for cultivating ideas; instead, she studied practical subjects, found a job in Denver, went to Milwaukee to work for a while, and then returned to a position in Denver. She never married. With bright auburn hair, a creamy complexion, lovely features, and a lively manner, she must have attracted many men. One of her suitors she simply didn't love. With another, she was certainly taken. He was a lawyer, who later became a judge. At some point in what appeared to be a courtship, the man's mother said to Margaret, "You know, George will never marry. He would never leave Jeanne [the sister] and me." This death knell to their courtship did not signal, however, the end of the relationship between Aunt Margaret and the family; she remained a close friend of Jeanne and the mother and saw George occasionally in the family setting. Many years later, George died. It was then discovered that the mother had spoken both truly and falsely. Truly—for George never moved from his home with his mother and sister. Falsely—for he *had* married. He and his secretary were wed secretly; but their tie remained unknown to any member of his family, and the only times they could be together at night were during the trips that he took, occasionally on judicial business for the state, more often to attend statewide or national legal meetings. What the arrangements were for disposal of his property at his death I do not know; but of course it was in connection with his inheritance that the secret marriage was discovered.

I do not know either what Aunt Margaret felt upon learning of this marriage. She continued to see the mother and sister; after the old woman's death, she was asked one day by Jeanne—not her elder—to come over and scrub the bathtub for her. To admit that she went to help will suggest that she was a moral simpleton. But that is not the case; she was, rather, an unusually good person, incapable of being unfeeling toward anyone in need, generous with all her family, kind to neighbors, including some who did not deserve it, and able to get along with even the most difficult co-workers (first at the *Rocky Mountain News,* later at the Denver office of the American Red Cross). She was often hurt by the indifferent and callous, even the cruel response to her generosity. And perhaps the experience with George did leave a scar. For when she died in 1982, she left equal portions of her estate to three nieces and a great-niece, but nothing at all to her one surviving nephew, toward whom, I am convinced, she harbored no resentment at all, but who was a *man.* As my cousin Beth Ann said, Aunt Margaret was a closet feminist.

She was one of many independent women in my family whom I have known or about whose lives some information has come down, going back to the previous century, and who were models of fortitude, ingenuity, and adaptability. Although they may not have known the word, some of them can rightly be called feminists—at least if moral and physical strength, self-reliance, and a sense of their own value help define that position, as the rhetoric of today's feminists implies. They were not, to be sure, militant, and they were not politicized; but only radicals believe, I suppose, that a woman's awareness of herself as an autonomous being must lead to militancy on behalf of others. Some lived without the support of husbands or fathers, wearing the pants as well as the apron.

One of these was my great-grandmother Sarilda Richardson Wright, born in Kentucky in 1821. By her first marriage, to a Mr. Lamberth, she had a son. When Lamberth died, she remarried, this time to a widower, Thomas Wright, with two children, of whom one was still at home. At some point they moved to Missouri. This union produced two more children; then, when they were quite young, Wright died, leaving a widow with three children of her own and a stepson. They were not people of great property, and, according to my mother, the Civil War was a time of particular hardship for them. To make ends meet, Sarilda raised sheep, sheared them, corded and washed the wool, and wove it into cloth, which she sold; and, as a girl, her elder daughter (my great-aunt Mag, born in 1849, I think, and whom I remember, since she lived until 1946) sewed at home by candlelight, making ruffles and other trinkets to sell. If this does not indicate resourcefulness, fortitude, and independence, I do not know what does.

That others of whom I shall speak were not so autonomous does not mean that they were underdeveloped creatures with warped personalities, psychologically and economically so dependent upon a spouse that they could not have survived otherwise; nor does it mean, to use a homely expression, that they always got the short end of the stick. Nor did these women necessarily believe that they labored under the servitude of what current feminists would define as sexism. *Labor,* yes—like American men, who, with rare exceptions, throughout the nineteenth and first half of the twentieth century worked for long hours, often at physically tasking jobs, without the assurance that the expected course of economic realities would continue to provide for their needs. But, for these women, labor was probably carried out with less of a sense of servitude than one finds among many women today.

Partly it was because, in some cases, they had no choice but to follow the structural and work patterns of their society and its economy. True freedom, Sartre argues, is the freedom to will what one has to do, not the license or the possibility simply to do what one wants. It was also for the very reason that they worked; as Voltaire so rightly observes at the end of *Candide,* work keeps away three evils—boredom, vice, and need. For both sexes, work was often less abstract than now (less mediated through money), and the products of labor were more easily gauged and valued. Another factor was that the sharing of labor was obvious; many more husbands and wives worked together, side by side, on a farm or some small enterprise. Furthermore, it was clear that women's labor was highly valued. When a first wife died, a man, with or without children, hastened to find a replacement. When Aunt Mag, who had no children (although she married twice), but helped raise her sister's children, spent her mornings doing the housework, washing, and cooking, then her afternoons at needlework (often mixed, happily, with the enjoyment of company), it was a significant contribution to the economy of family and society. There was also the fact that the men often sacrificed themselves, visibly, for their wives and children. When, in 1890, the other daughter of Sarilda and Thomas Wright, Susan, and her husband Arthur Stanforth, left Missouri, with their stable life and family connections, to go first to Kansas, then Colorado, it was because Susan had tuberculosis.

In short, I cannot believe that these women felt relative to the absolute of men; for much of what they did was the absolute of the time, being so closely associated with life itself. Beauvoir has argued that, contrary to what one would assume, women's reproductive role confines them to the relative, because it is repetitious, creative only in the biological sense (*re*production), whereas male work goes beyond biology to remake the world through invention (production). If there is truth in this observation, it nevertheless does not apply well to those nineteenth-century Americans for whom life and invention were nearly synonymous, as, on vast territories, they built a nation by the instruments of their very lives.

Let it not be thought, either, that all these women could perform was housework. Take, for instance, on the paternal side of my mother's family, a Mary Minerva Stanforth Curl. As one of the eldest children in a large family, she had early responsibilities, and "her girlhood education was very meager," as the newspaper obituary put it. But later, "by means of much study in spare moments, she fitted herself for the teaching profession and taught until the time of her marriage." Then there was Lydia Stanforth Pickens, who (I quote, again, from an obituary) "completing her preparation in the old Green City [Missouri] College, taught school in the district schools of this and adjoining counties for several years."

What distinguished these women, and many others of their time, most noticeably, in addition to their rectitude, was their dignity. They were proud, not with the arrogance that is condemned by Scripture but with a sense of their own honor and worth. Since pride is essentially a self-reflective virtue, it can be occasioned by almost anything: the poor are often as proud as the wealthy and

successful, sometimes more self-consciously so, since, as the saying goes, pride is all they have. The women I am portraying took
legitimate pride in their accomplishments and virtues—teaching,
homemaking skills, rearing of children, religious piety, and maintaining of relationships with family and the community at large.
As the newspaper said about Great-aunt Lydia:

> Mrs. Pickens has always been especially interested in the best
> things of life for her family, self-sacrificing at all times in
> their behalf, holding up before them the highest ideals and
> desiring for them the ability to take their place in life in an
> honorable and upright manner. She and her faithful compan-
> ion labored together through the years to the end, that as they
> came to the evening time of life, they could look with satis-
> faction upon the work of their hands.

(I do not know whether a local journalist or a family member
composed this piece. It is not, in any case, more fulsome than the
obituary of a small-town doctor I read just a few years ago, written, I suppose, by his offspring, or possibly by himself; the man
had left his wife at one point to run off—temporarily—with a
nurse, but you would have thought, from the article, that he was
a model husband and father as well as a research scientist and physician of great stature.) The contents of pride may be redefined by
cultural changes, but the sense of self-identity that it confers, or
reveals, remains the same: Aunt Mag was proud of her pie-making
skills, her beautifully designed quilts, her ability to wring a wet
sheet as dry as a wringer could; I find satisfaction in finishing a
well-crafted poem, a book, or an article with fifty footnotes. No
matter that I buy my pies from Mackenzie's Bakery, that my beds,
unlike hers, are made sometimes askew, and that I can barely hem
a pair of pants: what needs to be done in my life, according to its
responsibilities, gets done.

In the same generation as Aunt Mag and Aunt Lydia, there was
my paternal grandmother, who took a degree at Mt. Holyoke
College. Phoebe Elliott came from a moneyed family, however,
and did not work as a young woman. I have recounted earlier how,

afflicted with tuberculosis, she left Montreal, with her mother, and traveled by train and stagecoach to Saguache, Colorado, where she met and later married Edward Hill. She was stubbornly attached to her own ways. For instance, she never renounced her Canadian citizenship. What is more telling is the fact that, although she considered herself a Christian and attended church, she did not have any of her children baptized; it went against the grain for her to submit to authority in that way. Despite her devotion to Edward, she would not renounce her principles in culinary matters to please him: watermelon she considered too common to be brought into the house, and she refused to learn to bake lemon pies, so his daughters-in-law often served him these delicacies of the American heartland.

She raised her girls to be similarly independent. When her children were quite young, she visited Montreal with them; she sent the eldest there for a year of schooling during her adolescence. Both her daughters as well as their brothers attended college, pursued careers, traveled, had their own bank accounts—as did my grandmother herself. Yet her life was not always smooth, and she showed that could take the bitter with the sweet. Flora, her younger daughter, fell ill with rheumatic fever as a child and was bedridden for some seven years; caring for her, at the same time that five other children were in the household, must have been an enormous burden. But Phoebe lasted long and well; in her eighties, she could still vacuum the stairs with the heavy Hoover cleaner, which weighed almost as much as she did.

Although my position is contrary to that of the contemporary militant feminists—I always vote against them at faculty meetings and talk back to the television set when one of them rants on the evening news—I too am a sort of feminist in the cupboard, as are most of my friends, to one degree or another. (Well, one is scarcely in the cupboard now at all, although she remains married.) By this I mean that, on the one hand, we conform generally to social usages and operate from within the structure of the family, like the few women I know who do not work; but, on the other hand, having the same independent spirit and drive that characterized our predecessors, we have taken advantage of today's opportunities to lead a professional life, with its own choices and demands. We take care, variously, of husbands, children, aging parents, and see to house and garden, a choice of a university for son or daughter, and moral and civic responsibilities such as church activities, PTA, voter registration drives, and so on. We have our own beliefs, our own writing or painting or music, some of our own friends, and we expect the menfolk in our lives to accept them, as we accept theirs, and to give us of their time and acknowledge that today's duties are not yesterday's.

To live thus is not for *every* woman, any more than self-employment, risk, and originality are right, or possible, for every man. But it is nothing new; widespread now, I suspect it is as old as society, certainly as the society we know. The women authors who appeared in France as early as the twelfth century—as early as there were any writers at all—must have been so inclined, for, while they conformed to their time outwardly, they took upon themselves the creative and even the amorous roles of men, identifying themselves with and by their literary calling and writing love lyrics in which the sexual roles are reversed. Two centuries later, Christine de Pizan argued for equality of the sexes in the context of universal human values. Louise Labé, a Renaissance writer from Lyons, adopted men's dress to follow an army, then returned to Lyons, married, but took a lover, another poet, with whom she exchanged beautiful love lyrics. In the early seventeenth century, Marie de Gournay, Montaigne's intellectual heir and the editor of his *Essays,* published a treatise on the equality of men and women; in the following century, several women writers adopted positions that would now be recognized as feminist, including Madeleine de Puisieux, author of the treatise *Woman Is Not Inferior to Man;* and yet most of these writers were married women.

The cupboard is useful, in any case. Conformity is like clothes, which conceal one's intimate self (which should not be paraded indiscriminately before others) and, unless one's dress is eccentric, signify that one admits to belonging to one's sex, place, and time, and perhaps one's class or profession. Under this semblance, however, one can exercise all sorts of freedom, and even get away with subversiveness, because no one suspects it. Of course I am speaking from the perspective of someone who does not desire a new sexual revolution to usher in the coming millenium. True revolutionaries must abandon any pretense of conformity, usually of legality, in order to confront directly and aggressively the structures, laws, or mores that they deem unacceptable and enroll others in a campaign, underground or open, to destroy these structures.

Is it they only who are consistent with their positions? Does the middle ground between the traditional view of the inferiority (or at least the restricted roles and rights) of women and current militant feminism imply a hypocritical, or certainly an incoherent, reconciliation of opposites? The whole question of wisdom arises in this connection. Those Greeks who held up the ideal of the golden mean, and their neoclassical imitators in the early modern period, were *men*. Their thinking arose in a society that was familiar with political turmoil and military threats but whose fundamental (and elitist) structures were stable. It was a thinking geared not to change but to maintaining institutions and values within a cycle of repetition (natural and political). The idea of moderation reflected, appropriately, the need for balancing and offsetting the pressures that could threaten order.

Yet their conclusions laid claim to universality, like those of the eighteenth-century political philosophers in Europe and America who contributed, indirectly or directly, to the shaping of our republic. What is more important, it is within this very intellectual tradition of universality that extremists ordinarily operate, at least in the Occident. What happens is that the mean, without losing its central position, has been gradually displaced in the direction of what can be termed liberalization. It can be argued, then, that the idea of mean is essential, constituting a necessary position along the spectrum of ideas; it is not merely a soft position for those who wish, as the French saying puts it, to satisfy both the goat and the cabbage, but rather is a legitimate moral and intellectual stance.

None of this rationalization is really required for one to adopt *any* position; anyway, we live our lives viscerally as well as intellectually, in response to a situation. I know a woman from Texas who, in the 1940s, not long after she married, moved with her husband to a mining compound in New Mexico, in country so desolate that by contrast the little town of Silver City seemed like a metropolis. Accustomed to cities, with their cultural stimulation and their opportunities for social intercourse, she was appalled by the wildness and isolation she found; and she felt that her husband, a talented surgeon, belonged more in a major hospital than in a community of miners, where the only person, in addition to her, with whom he could have any sort of intellectual conversation was the Catholic priest. But, as she tells it, she came to realize that, since he had chosen to work there, she too must choose the place; she saw it as opportunity, not exile, and came to love those he assisted and with whom she, as a nurse, assisted him. Neither she nor others, certainly, would think of her as a feminist; yet her choice was as constructive for her as for him, and the whole life that came out of it was authentic.

In my view, the true feminist will have a firm sense of her own value and that of her sex, analogous to the sense a man has of his worth as a male, each sex feeling and living through its identity, as through the body and situation in general. The true feminist must be also a universalist, since it is in the context of common, shared values that her uniqueness is identified. I am aware that one school of thought, fed by anthropology and sociology, denies the possibility of universal values, arguing that there are only particulars. If this were strictly true, there would be no communication, no society, no philosophy; all would be atomistic. What is really meant is that the objectors feel neglected or threatened as individuals by the appeal to common values, and fear that abstractions will cover over concrete cases. Justified in some circumstances, certainly, these objections are ill-suited to today's intellectual woman, a product (to a great extent) of the universalism that opened schools and professions.

Today is New Year's Day, a suitable time for taking stock. After I finish writing this, I shall go down to the kitchen and put my apron over my blue jeans, once the insignia of my girlish effort at making myself according to *my* idea and not society's, now so associated with both sexes, after the erosion of certain vestimentary codes, that they are merely a sign of casual dressing. While my husband, awaiting the Bowl games, meditates in his rocking chair, I shall open for lunch a can of mushroom soup, his favorite—I prefer tomato. (Breaking with tradition, we do not eat black-eyed peas, which taste like muddy water.) I shall reflect on how we both have reached a mean, his and mine being not identical but close. Whereas his mother kept house and went out into society, wearing a frock, a hat, and white gloves (I have a picture of her from the *Times-Picayune,* dressed to the nines for a tea), I go to the office every day and wear, variously, jeans, slacks, or tailored suits; whereas she prepared red beans and rice by the slow-cooking method while doing the wash and hanging out clothes on Mondays, and baked cakes from scratch, I use canned beans, patronize Mackenzie's, and dry our clothes in an electric machine.

But, far from minding, my husband expects this from me, always granting that I should spend as much time as I wish poking around in the library or writing. This represents a displacement, by him, the conservative, from a traditionalist view to a liberated one—but at small cost, really, since he has few wants anyhow and does not care to pursue all the corresponding male traditions as represented by his father. For my part, although I have much freedom to do as I wish, I have to locate my mean close enough to tradition to allow for serving his dinner six days a week at 6:30 promptly, preparing pot roast frequently although I don't like it, doing all the laundry and grocery shopping, and granting him much authority in such matters as when we leave for the Rendon Inn on Fridays and whom we should invite to our party. This conciliation of our individual positions and interests has served us well; before another afternoon to be spent at the computer keyboard or settled with my books in my sybaritic chair, I'll go heat the soup.

On Grace

In the last of the evening light, the desert seems to be drawing into itself, the hot blood of the day cooled, the skin of the earth contracting, colors muted, but sounds keener, as if alert. The Las Animas mountain range has abandoned its blue for its mysterious nocturnal shadow. From the terrace of Frances and J.C.'s ranch-style house, we drink leisurely draughts of the approaching night, with its serene beauty, its gentleness. The sky is poised over the darkening landscape like gauze, which an early star pins up like a veil and where the winds pass freely.

This is the last evening that my daughter and I will spend with my cousin Frances and her husband, J.C., an affable West Texan, in Deming, in the southwest corner of New Mexico. The following day they will put us on the Sunset Limited for El Paso and then New Orleans. Our visit has been uneventful, the entertainment certainly not lavish. In fact, since Frances is usually in a wheelchair because of her arthritis, it is the guests who have helped J.C. prepare the meals and clean up afterwards. Our diversions have been inspecting J.C.'s garden, with its squash, tomatoes, and fruit trees; watching the Cubs on TV (since Deming has no station of its own, it is hyper-cabled, with stations from Los Angeles to Chicago); riding to K-Bob's Steak House for a meal; and visiting Pancho Villa State Park and Las Palomas, a tacky town in Old Mexico, across from Columbus. Yet, this evening, as we let the sense of the desert approach and surround us, I am almost possessed by it and the rest of the setting—or rather, by what inhabits it and which I am going to call, for the moment at least, *grace*.

While not a novelty, the term may appear startling. Short of theologians—among whom I do not count myself—who speaks of it nowadays? True, in a few families the word appears at mealtimes, in the blessing at table—a custom not entirely lost, particularly among some New Orleans families I know, who count members of religious orders in their number and take pride in a long tradition of Catholicism in the city, going back at least to the founding of the Ursuline convent in 1727. (Some of these people still say their blessing in French.) Grace remains, also, a standard of social behavior, at least for some—though nowadays it occurs frequently in reference to a situation where someone has *avoided* a social obligation or deftly skirted an awkwardness: "Well, you certainly got out of that gracefully." Until two or three decades ago, moreover, when changes in manners and deportment made slouching acceptable and drove the waltz and even the fox-trot from the dance floor, one heard such comments as "She walks with grace" or "That couple dances gracefully."

Graciousness was then as desirable as *gracefulness,* and the two were associated by more than their common lexical element in the minds of those who believed that "Pretty is as pretty does," that grace of exterior person bespoke—or should bespeak, if it is genuine—an inner quality partaking of generosity, kindness, tact, and compassion. Perhaps it was both form and content that Hemingway wished to suggest in his famous "grace under pressure." Similarly, when one speaks of grace in writing—these days the occasion arises seldom, unfortunately—does the term not suggest a quality that goes beyond mere ornament of style and felicitous expression to indicate something in the heart of the writing? If it be thought that Keats's Romantic equivalence of truth and beauty is sloppy, that rhetoric is something to beware of, I would answer: it depends on the rhetoric. One has only to think of the axiom of that legislator of French classicism, Boileau, for whom clarity of mind and felicity of expression were one:

> Ce que l'on conçoit bien s'énonce clairement,
> Et les mots pour le dire arrivent aisément.

A few other uses persist—grace notes, for instance, a term used well before Mozart's time, to indicate a note that a composer wished to write in but that musical usage of the day forbade including in the main melody line because it was not a harmonic note (did not belong properly to the chord below it). Think, too, of the Three Graces, whom classical-minded readers still cherish as the three goddesses who had control over pleasure and beauty (and for one of whom, Thalia, a street in New Orleans quite near me is named, I am pleased to say). Then there is "grace period," a term used surely with increasing frequency, since it is not only the inability of people to pay what they owe that seems to have grown, but also their desire to do so. The antonym of the word under examination, *disgrace*, still suggests offense to the eye ("My office is a disgrace," I say, gesturing to strewn books and papers) and often to the moral sense.

Grace also means clemency, and while the use does not appear frequently in American speech, it is still a part of French legal parlance, one with a venerable history, going back to the days when kings such as Saint Louis under his oak rendered justice and sometimes pardoned malefactors. I suppose a few women are still named Grace—and Grace Kelly is occasionally shown on the cover of supermarket tabloids (doubtless without the comment that the name particularly fitted someone who married a prince)—but in a generation that will no longer be the case, suburban names such as Heather and Tiffany and even Brandy (!) having completely driven out the abstractions favored in previous centuries in America and having even begun to usurp the place of traditional appellations such as Helen and Jean. A *very* few people are, I suppose, still addressed as "Your Grace" in ecclesiastical and royal courts.

Yet all these uses, some of which are rather marginal, cannot, even together, come close to having the encompassing power that the word had for centuries and still has for those whose belief is accompanied by an examination of the human situation in which that faith operates. More germane to my purposes here, none of the uses quite fits the circumstances I alluded to earlier, for which, nonetheless, the word *grace* seems so apt. Perhaps, then, one needs to have recourse to the theological suggestions after all, even when it is a question of an evening in the desert.

Or should I say *especially* when it concerns an evening in the desert? Although as a Palestinian he must have been familiar with barren country and surely passed through some on his wanderings, Saint Paul, that supreme apostle and exponent of grace, was, to be sure, a man of towns. But John the Baptist, Saint Jerome, Saint Simon, and countless other holy men and women took up their habitations in the wilderness, in which they seemed to find strength in proportion to the desolation. Didn't Saint Anthony also go to the desert? Saint John, whose name means, if I am not mistaken, "God is gracious," is one of my favorites. He is both the recipient and the announcer of divine favor, the voice crying in the wilderness of a great and gracious coming.

Even agnostics have repaired to the desert to search for the only share of grace allowed them. In an early essay Camus speaks of the serenity, even in the face of death, that comes in the desolate North African landscape, where one is "a stone among stones." In *The Stranger*, his hero, Meursault, whom he called in a preface "the only saint whom we deserve," is almost a man of the Algerian desert; the humanitarian Dr. Rieux, in *The Plague*, looks out from the prison of Oran to the desert and mountains to the south, which represent freedom ("grace"); the hero of Camus's story "The Guest," who says that he could not really live outside of the North African desert and its stones, offers to a prisoner a clemency that is refused, and for which he himself will be mercilessly punished.

I think I have made my point: something in the vast and arid spaces, in their silence and barrenness, speaks to us, still, even through routines and circumstances that are far from exceptional, while at the same time suggesting the rigors, even the tragedy of the human condition. In the case of the experience evoked earlier, however, there were other elements also that contributed to the sense of grace. One was a feeling of utter comfort. My cousin Frances, it should be specified, is an entire generation older than I, though our mothers were sisters; her daughter was born before me. My own mother, deceased by the time of the visit, had helped her sister raise Frances and four other children; now, in my middle age, Frances, returning the favor, took on something of a maternal role for me, simply by being there. I could know, at last, something of the grace that comes by being a child—by having been given, gratuitously, to parents and the world—but which the *child* is unable to feel and comprehend; and, with my own daughter, I was sensitive as well to the grace that comes from having a child. It was, in a word, like being again in the small home my parents had established in arid West Texas—a home that otherwise was gone, existing only in my mind.

The simplicity of our days was similarly comfortable. What would have been boredom in other circumstances because it would not have fit them was, instead, the very expression and essence of our purpose: we were, after all, *on vacation*. This vacancy would be intolerable to me ordinarily; we have not been put here to do nothing. Beauvoir recounts an incident from Plutarch in which Pyrrhus recites to Cineas his ambitious plans for future conquest. When he says that afterwards he will rest, Cineas replies, "Why not rest immediately?" The meaning, clearly, is in the conquest, not the repose. But it is well that the rhythm of human activity be broken by moments of introspection, retrospection, and prospection, and of a kind of discipline that consists in putting aside for a time one's projects. Some would call this meditation, others prayer; monkish routines were established in part to favor such. Now our routine in Deming was not ascetic—we had soft beds, good steaks, and bourbon-and-water before dinner—but it was leisurely, inviting to affectionate fellowship with others and pleasant company with oneself.

The tour I have made around the word *grace* has involved such detours, and has drawn such a wide circle, that all sorts of other things would appear to have been included in the experience to which I refer, and in the concept. Indeed, it is not a simple notion, even theologically. It involves liberality or freedom: salvation, as the Apostle insists and the evangelicals repeat after him, is *freely* given through divine goodness, and must also be freely received— that is, received by an act of the will. Even though there is less evidence for this in Scripture, I believe it involves also economy, propriety, and order. Economy, in the theological sense that God does not dissipate grace, and in the esthetic sense, for true beauty and grace cannot involve prolixity or excessive ornamentation of any type: even grace notes have their function. Propriety, for some of the same reasons: ornamentation improperly added is no longer beautiful; grace misplaced would no longer be grace, but a travesty thereof. (This does not mean that kings and others may not have pardoned some who probably did not deserve it; indeed, the current governor of Louisiana has made such errors in full knowledge. But then his act is not, properly speaking, clemency, but favoritism.) As for order, we are told (again, speaking theologically) that the redemption is *in order*, part of the drama of which the Divinity is the director; and, in terms of esthetics, manners, anything you will, disorderly grace is a contradiction.

All these notions—to which one could add beauty, but that goes without saying, part of the dictionary definition—adhere to the sense of grace that surrounds me. Three women, of three generations, compose a biological and social order that we acknowledge as fundamental. Recognizing our dependency on it does not necessarily lead to melancholy. Bernanos argues that the child's sense of well-being is coextensive with his entire dependency on his mother. The acknowledgment of one's place in time has a certain reassurance to it; even death can, like the dry bones in the sand, seem part of order. Similarly, to me, at least, propriety is clear here, according to Montaigne's dictum that "the grand and glorious masterpiece of man is to learn how to live *a propos*," for Frances and J.C. have, with each other, recognized what is fitting and possible for two people of their age and have designed their daily life accordingly. Economy is everywhere present: and I am not speaking of thrift (though that too is a virtue) but of disposition of time, strength, and assets—of husbandry.

And all these notions can be related to the desert, where their form is visible in the unbroken sun of day and the stark, barren night and from which sprang the idea, indeed the name, of oasis. The balance of nature is so delicate, so carefully ordered, and everything is so *a propos* that it seems like an object lesson. In *Wind, Sand, and Stars*, Antoine de Saint-Exupéry tells how the fennecs (small desert foxes) in North Africa meticulously drink the morning dew on the stones and eat the snails that have appeared on the spindly plants—being careful, however, never to eat so much from one area that the food supply will be threatened. Say what you want about English gardens: they cannot come nearly so close to suggesting paradise as can a few fruit trees planted in the sandy soil, watered by sparse rain or the deep grace of wells, producing through nature's finest economy, and against the expectations of everyone except those who know the place, amazing abundance. There is even grace in so much light, so much lucidity—at least if one considers that the principle of darkness is kin to obscurantism, disorder, abandon, and despair.

I make no claim to live always in this way; it must have been precisely because I do not that the sense of grace could touch me on Frances and J.C.'s terrace. *They* are in it and perhaps do not know it fully; a certain type of beatitude does not require conscious assent. Outside of it, I see its strength. Grace is elsewhere, too, of course; the reader will surely want to supply examples. The music of Bach, for instance, vibrating, swelling like a full river with the most severe, yet profound feelings of order, beauty, liberality—indeed, freedom. I think of a homely example also: birds singing in the trees near my window. Saint Francis saw it that way, too, but I shall add on the matter an observation he could not have made. Men have made things in some sense more wondrous than a bird—for instance, the powerful birds with aluminum wings that take us (faster than sound, in some cases—and at altitudes the birds cannot begin to reach) across the ocean in a few hours. And people may make things more wondrous still, perhaps redoing the human being through genetic engineering. But *men would not have thought of making a sparrow or a cardinal.* Now that they are here, of course we "think" them as part of the order we expect. But I can quite imagine that, since they serve no purpose but their own, we would not have invented them if they didn't exist, unlike Voltaire's God. Part of the natural economy and order, they are serendipitous—given through nature's liberality.

Many things devised and reproduced by human beings are quite without grace, in any sense—most buildings, most manufactured objects, much else that assails our eyes and ears. Some creations of engineering are striking exceptions: I am thinking of cathedrals, ships, and bridges in particular. Who would deny beauty of line and ornamentation to the great Romanesque basilica of Vézelay and to Gothic cathedrals such as those in Paris and Chartres? Elaborate though they are, they have their own order and economy, surely—even, paradoxically, a sort of simplicity—and propriety both esthetic and spiritual. Their very existence seems a grace: that such immense and moving structures could have been imagined, to start with, and then built without power-driven machinery, and then endure to our day gives to history, bloody though it be, a wondrous and redeeming dimension of power and spirituality.

Ships, identified with war since the *Iliad* and connected to much human loss and grief, are yet generally thought of as beautiful, and are associated with freedom because they manifest particularly well the human project of pressing on, exploring, conquering nature. Particularly attractive is their movement through water, which is resistant (power is required) and yet is not solid, calling attention perhaps to the ambiguity of the human condition, where (as the existentialists would have it, at least) we are thrown into a world whose resistance is both a threat and a motivation to action. As for bridges, if one's view is arrested by everything from a simple railroad trestle or footbridge to the Golden Gate span by San Francisco Bay, and even that populist bridge over the Mississippi at New Orleans, named for Huey P. Long, is it because the idea of *bridging*—again, conquering nature, reuniting for human benefit and by an act of freedom what nature had separated—is particularly appealing?

Grace is not, however, *everywhere*. Leaving aside the great evils of our time, which clearly are contrary to all propriety and order, properly speaking, and which, if anything, bespeak satanic forces, one can readily identify all sorts of structures and activities from which grace seems singularly lacking. One I should like to propose is deconstructionism, a cultural construct (one would say anti-construct, except that it coheres in its own perverted way and has proven both monolithic and totalitarian, its adherents evidently supposing that even if all *other* texts have no determinable meaning, its own do) that denies literary and linguistic coherence—that is, order; undermines the economy of the text; and challenges the validity of esthetic pleasure and the appropriateness of much that has been called culture. If you need persuading, just read some of the prose of Jacques Derrida and de Man and so on, and say whether in any way, content or form, the notion of grace, as I have proposed it, can be found there in the least. The theologically minded will agree with my challenge if they reflect that, in denying to language the possibilities of referentiality and meaning, the deconstructionists are denying that Word which the Gospel of Saint John puts at the beginning of its text, and at the beginning of time.

Now perhaps this notion of grace will be judged, *ipso facto*, out of style and useless, harmful even, if it cannot incorporate what to some is one of the greatest intellectual creations of the twentieth century. It might be regarded as is the law, frequently and rightly: if it excludes or denies what should be included and acknowledged, according to contemporary views on justice and morality, or if it distorts what is perceived presently as truth, it should be abandoned. Or, perhaps more aptly, the scientific analogy might be called upon. Erroneous understandings of the planet and heavens and their contents have been discarded as scientific speculation and experimentation have devised or discovered explanations and truths we deem more accurate; having put away (pseudo-scientific) childish things, we should similarly discard those false idols, such as meaning, to which de Man and company have drawn our attention.

Various arguments can be summoned against these positions. Unlike legislation, conditioned by the time and social circumstances, great moral and spiritual truths are transhistorical; the best thought of the past retains its validity, and although Socrates' world view is outmoded, his ethics are not. The idea of progress in moral thought and understanding—or in religious belief, if you are of that mind—is quite different from the notion of scientific progress. Even if the inner spirit of each individual should, by the old puritan standard at least, be the stage for endless striving toward moral improvement, it must be rebegun for each: no one can progress for another. Most readers will doubtless recognize, anyway, that as a whole the human race is still struggling to make improvements that are both lasting and generalized; certainly, barbarity has not disappeared.

The old ideas, then, are hardly outworn when it comes to things moral. Similarly with esthetics: the Greek sculptures and vases I admire at the Chicago Art Institute and similar museums are here to attest to it. Moreover—and here I am going to venture far in my thinking—grace and graciousness, in all the senses I identified, really belong to that larger area of human endeavor that is at the root of cultural history as we know it: the attempt at once to live the human condition, in all its contradictions, and to go beyond it. They are the source, perhaps the sign, of this going-beyond—a transformation that does not deny life but works within it. Think merely of the cultural import of dancing, which, whether religious, erotic, or funereal (as in jazz funerals in New Orleans), by multiplying the body's grace and separating it from utilitarian functionalism, helps to divest it of its animality and invests it with a going-beyond that denies its limitations in mere reproduction and death. The literature of the past, by which some writers expressed grace in the soul, others gracefulness in language and form, and still others both, speaks still of this effort to transcend. Certainly, grace and graciousness are the opposite of nihilism, and nihilism (to return to the position I am opposing) is what deconstructionism and other denials of grace lead to. Let it take what form you please, dance, music, poetry, cathedral, prayer, friendship, passion (for it too is a transcendence), or simply a long summer's evening in the New Mexico sands: the burden of being and thinking, like the body's gravity, can become light in the presence of grace.

On Living

$\mathcal{H}$aving done a considerable amount of it by now, I want to look at the activity to which we are born and which most of us pursue more or less vigorously—living. Montaigne tells how a man suffering nearly all the afflictions to which the flesh is heir asked (rhetorically, it turns out), "Who will deliver me from these ills?" When it was pointed out that he had deliverance in his power—in the form of suicide—he retorted, "I asked who will deliver me from these ills, not from life itself." For, even in grief and sickness, the mind and the body usually cling to their existence, their welfare, and their self-identity. Surely among the strangest of diseases is depression, impairing as it does the desire to protect and prolong existence, a desire that is usually integral to life and without which the species and individuals thereof would not have made it thus far.

In my case, a strong physical drive to activity and commitment to the business of living have offset—happily, I suppose—some depressive tendencies in the mind. When I was young, my father cited the *joie de vivre* displayed by a calf at play in a pasture, or our dog greeting us with leaps and wet kisses, then curling peacefully at our feet, and suggested that I approach life with the same immediacy and placidity. Unfortunately, I could not always follow this sage advice, any more than he could himself. As I have grown older and lost some of those I love, the tendencies toward melancholy have become more marked; conversely, my ability to deal with them and answer gloom with cheer has increased.

Why should this be so, and why should one fall into melancholy in the first place? I accept neither the strictly psychological nor the purely physical explanations for mental phenomena. The Freudian schema of a mysterious hidden self, manifested by disorders of the body but disguised and repressed deep within it, beyond the reach of "physick," even as it tyrannizes consciousness, strikes me as a fiction that raises more questions than it answers. Yet to equate all consciousness, or "soul," with the brain and nerve system that make it possible, and see human thought as merely the product of neuron activity, is not satisfactory either. The old joke says, "Is life worth living? It depends on the liver." Well, I will agree this much with some of the doctors of the psyche: that to cease wanting to live bespeaks, or is tantamount to, illness. The great sickness is death itself, but it is also a healer, removing often at its approach the desire as well as the possibility for prolonging life. If civilization and its discontents (what Freud called "the spread of neurasthenia") contribute to the sickness of depression, truly they constitute a sort of collective malady.

Civilization, as Freud defined it in his famous essay, is "the whole sum of the achievements and the regulations that distinguish our lives from those of our animal ancestors and that serve two purposes—namely to protect men against nature and to adjust their mutual relations." He has in mind, of course, the achievements of technology and science, and such abstractions as beauty and justice, but especially the development of the libido, the sense of guilt, and so on. I would prefer to define civilization broadly but more pointedly as the organizations and products of the animal that knows it is going to die. That death is mysteriously fascinating to us does not require the postulation of a universal death wish; it speaks more to the powerful drive to live, deeply and properly disturbed by its opposite. In this light, culture is by definition allied to discontent; thought—the awareness of mortality—is its inspirer and enabler. (Think of religion and of art—since every type of graphic and plastic art, from the animals drawn with charcoal on the cave walls in Lascaux and the Anasazi petroglyphs to the great Gothic cathedrals, seems to be connected to the threat of death. Or, if you wish, think simply of funeral repasts.) "Man is unhappy because he thinks," says Gisors in Malraux's *Man's Fate*. But, within this awareness and as an aspect of it, the human animal continues, stubbornly if not always with grounding in reflection, to prolong its existence. Some, perhaps instinctively, on the model of the beasts, perhaps through considered choice, make

existence its own sufficient reason. In the *Essays,* someone complained that he had done nothing the whole day. "What!" answered Montaigne. "You have lived!" The analytical question of
means versus end is thus cut like the Gordian knot by a synthetic
view that sees life as a whole, process and product, means and end.

What does this have to do with me, or any other individual? To
philosophize, wrote the author of the *Essays,* is to learn how to
die. Millions live without such reflection, and, whether they do it
through natural indolence and serenity or because they are too oc-
cupied with meeting basic daily needs to have the luxury of abstract thinking, they may be closer than philosophers suspect to
certain things in heaven and earth. But, born to a sort of question-
ing malaise, I cannot live only in that way, and Socrates' dictum
that the unexamined life is not worth living holds for me great
validity. Even if living suffices unto itself, it must be lived *as
thought* also. Moreover, I am convinced that the other side of the
coin of reflection—reflection's ability to turn back on itself, a critical circle from which there is no escape and which can be madden-
ing—is, ultimately, comforting: the anguish of being—which may
arise prior to reflection but is sharpened by it—has as part of its
own awareness the consciousness of its limitations.

Such limitations of anguished reflection are multiple. One is the
knowledge that this too shall pass away. Another comes from
mind's relation to the cosmos (or chaos) at large: how ridiculous
that this little mote of thought should attempt to encompass, comprehend, and declare itself an absolute in the immense universe to
which twentieth-century physics has introduced us. (And not just
recent physics. Pascal made the very same point in the seventeenth
century.) A third limitation of angst is relative to its own authen-
ticity, as verified by will. I shall not make light of those who do
indeed carry anguish to its extreme conclusion by ending their life:
socially and perhaps existentially speaking, such is deplorable. But
their numbers are exceeded by those who claim life holds neither
meaning nor interest for them but who, in the midst of their cyni-
cism and complaints, gratify themselves most anti-nihilistically.
The example of Schopenhauer, praising suicide at the head of a

groaning board, is famous. Less so is that of my husband, who often says, in the midst of his gloom, that nothing holds him to life, but who will not get in an airplane for fear of dying in a crash.

Similarly, in Sartre's *Nausea*, Roquentin discovers that there is absolutely no reason for living; yet, in the form of an assemblage of heart, liver, stomach, bowels, and so forth, he keeps it up, letting his little thoughts simmer along and even going so far as to feel pleasure now and then. On a more abstract plane, there is the position of Camus, one of whose chief points in *The Myth of Sisyphus* is that, even though life has no meaning, it does not follow that one should not live. Dare I say, without seeming supercilious, that no one more than Camus was gratified by beautiful women, the companionship of friends, the pleasures of an evening spent in a café, a game of soccer, a good performance of his play, and even . . . fame?

Reflection, then, even in the form of anguish, need not be an impediment to living, and can be an enhancer of life, even as it is aware of the end to which both will come. My mind, Valéry points out, contains the world, which contains my mind; *my mind contains my mind*. Along with the capacity for symbolizing (including linguistically), this is one of the most astonishing things about human thought. Turned outward, the latter can embrace—or construct, if one prefers—so much of what we call the world; turned inward, it seizes as such its own apprehension of the world. Experience is multiplied by memory and contemplation; past and future, the one often decried as inauthentic, the other vaguely dreaded, release to the present their capacity for bestowing temporal meaning. Language, by reflecting and expressing experience, makes it communicable to the self in a way that the unmediated moment could not be, and communicable to multitudes. (I shall not claim that criticism comes then as a superior layer on top of literature to magnify it, in turn. Criticism is the servant of literature, not vice versa, as recent theorists seem to believe.)

Should, then, one live to think? Should one live to write (or paint, if that is one's medium)? The number of artists who seem to have done so is considerable. Hemingway has been accused, I believe, of selecting his adventures with a view toward writing them up. It is possible that Baudelaire maintained his relationship with Jeanne Duval in order to make poetry out of it; and painters have sometimes chosen as mistresses those who would also serve— for a time—as models. In his latter years, Proust appears to have consented to "live"—to go out in society, visit a museum, see friends—only to gather raw material for his masterpiece. But in his case, at least, this was pursued on the foundation of an enormous amount of genuine living. Surely his first excursions into society, his quarrels with his parents, his numerous liaisons with other young men and flirtations with women, his visits to Gothic cathedrals and trip to Venice were not undertaken merely as experiments with which to make a book; he wrote through and on account of such experiences, and his powerful imagination operated on a canvas of a world in which he had been engaged.

To seek out life merely with the end in mind of turning it into written reflection is, then, probably morally unsound—a type of esthetic imperialism. It is inauthentic and may lead also to very shallow art. There have been few child literary geniuses (Rimbaud is an exception); even when great lyrical gifts are present early, their development requires the maturation of experience, and the experience should be genuine: life is not easily fooled. Yet perhaps, instinctively, the artist does gravitate to the sort of experiences that he needs. Travel I have spoken of earlier. Love in particular— rarely sought out deliberately, but almost always existentially accepted—is useful for the intensity of feeling it provides, the acuteness of understanding of the self and other to which it sometimes leads, and—as Baudelaire and Proust, among others, would observe—the short and sure route it provides to suffering, that scalpel of the soul.

I will not deny that, in some obscure way, I may have been drawn to what would move me most deeply—which is not always the stable, the rational—and that, as a writer, being so moved has served me. Unhappiness and disorder have some deep appeal (it hurts me to write this, though, since neatness and regularity also are essential to me). Although such an attraction suggests a moral perversion, it is not without theological ratification. Salvation came after the fall; grace would be meaningless without sin. The

Catholic poet Pierre Jean Jouve built some powerful devotional lyrics around the idea of disorder as a moral necessity. Psychologically speaking, a pure mental unity is inconceivable. Consider perception, in which monotone or monochrome stimuli hold little interest and even cease to be perceived; likewise, cognition proceeds by distinctions and negations. Why should experience, then, not similarly thrive on changes and opposites—especially since the body itself, while retaining its identity, undergoes both short-term and long-term modifications? A full life of order can be built only on an understanding of disorder as a potentiality; and for understanding, there must be experience. Years ago my friend Patricia Teed was asked by someone (they were both in their mid-twenties), "Tell me, what is it like to be unhappy?" Without wishing to suggest that the speaker could not measure the value of her serene life—how can I know?—I will observe that the fabric of my own life, as I see it now, has been greatly dependent upon the experience of disorder and unhappiness of various sorts (my own and that of others, which mine has taught me to recognize and sympathize with). If this has led to a better-developed moral sense, so much the better; and if to think and write this life means more esthetic fullness also, it is because poetry in its fullness can come only from the personal dialectics of such experience. (Yeats said it before me.)

What, then, is good living? Saint Paul, I believe, spoke of being *in* the world but not *of* it. Except for monks and hermits, who have dialogue only with God (and whose condition I am not able to discuss), the rest of us are certainly *in* the world and mostly *of* it. It is better to recognize this. The world is our field, and I prefer a latitudinous interpretation of *world,* in all its variety. Connoisseurship and the snobbish insistence upon nothing but the best—from table china and men's shoes to concert seats and a university name—create an artificial standard that, by implication, denies value to anything shared with the multitudes—that is, to most of the human condition itself. No wonder that there is often a marked malaise in the lives of the very wealthy, the very privileged (a malaise that goes beyond the failure of material goods to produce satisfaction); for, no matter what they do to assert their separateness, reminders of their common humanity intrude upon them, in the form of social and political vexations and, more grievously, of illness, unhappiness, and death. As many a scene in films and novels has shown, at such time the abandoned or bereaved finds comfort in the consolations of a faithful servant, whose experience has, precisely, been shaped by such grief. Stripped to the skin of human fact, the elite and the common are the same.

Now this does not mean that human undertakings should be reduced only to the common denominator, still less that vulgarity is the yardstick. And what I have written will not suffice to justify to everyone some of my own common tastes—for country music, roadside cafés, Tex-Mex food, and NFL football games, for instance. (The violence of the latter, matched by the coarseness of the crowd, is a topic of criticism among the enlightened; but from what I have seen of history, this is very paltry stuff indeed, and we can probably absorb it without much moral damage—especially since the hypothesis that it syphons off some natural human aggressivity is not wholly without merit.) But imagine someone who could not endure any of the above popular tastes, or similar ones, and let me know whether you would care to be a close friend or the spouse of that person.

Yet, assuming that one has opportunities to do otherwise, living nothing but the common life is an impoverishment, as I suggested earlier. While I respect the humanity in a waitress I knew and her husband, I deplore, for instance, their inability to find entertainment in anything more sophisticated than a Saints' game or a monster truck-pull in the Superdome. (The limitations of the man in question have become such a household byword that we regularly speak of his type as a "Roy-like man.") To read a book more demanding than a Stephen King novel, to listen to a piece of music other than rock, to assess facts with care or follow a serious argument are all beyond them. They will never enter a museum, unless it be the Wax Museum in the French Quarter. Now surely, they do not care for their son any less than I care for my daughter; but what is to be done with the life for which they care is another matter.

What I am arguing for as a dimension of living is a type of self-consciousness, not the social but the metaphysical variety. (To refuse to eat an ice cream cone or a hot dog in the street because others are watching and proper people would not approve is foolish, as is any excessive concern with others' judgment in general. This criticism does not, however, imply license to arrive late, talk in the theater, throw litter in the street, and so forth. I have to confess, moreover, that I care about the clothes I put on my back—though more for esthetic than social reasons—and would wear a matronly "half-size" dress only to save a life or for some other compelling cause.) Now it is not proven that poetry and philosophy can save lives—nor is it proven, for that matter, that prayer can do so. Yet, as William Carlos Williams wrote in "Asphodel, That Greeny Flower":

> It is difficult
> to get the news from poems
>   yet men die miserably every day
>   for lack
> of what is found there.

One doesn't have to be Matthew Arnold, at least, to believe that lives can be *enlightened* and *intensified* by poetry and reflection—and this is true, or could be, for those of the most modest condition as well as the loftiest, for the great thing about thought is that it puts out what is put into it, and thus rarely exceeds the thinker's capacity.

The question of health arises in this connection. Is robust health an impediment or a blessing to creativity and reflection? Gide, citing such cases as Saint Paul, Rousseau, Dostoevsky, and his own, toyed with the idea that artistic or moral genius is the result of an imbalance—more precisely, the *righting* of an imbalance. Pascal carried on his meditations, scientific work, and apologetics by means of a sickly body, which gave out on him long before his due and which may have contributed to what some consider unparalleled moral genius and others (including Voltaire) call perversions of the mind. Proust, and Baudelaire, too, created out of moral and physical suffering. Yet two towering geniuses in nineteenth-century France, Balzac and Hugo, were powerfully healthy; doubtless only because of prolonged abuse of caffeine and too-intensive labor did Balzac barely go past the half-century mark. If talent is a given, creation springs from an adaptation of this given to circumstances, including the condition of the self; so that there can be genius in both sickness and health.

In any case, we mortals would be fools to remain indifferent to what the body can contribute to good living. How, living in New Orleans, could I be unaware of the refined pleasures of food and drink? In other cities, people talk to visitors about what to see or buy; here we talk about what and where to *eat*. Yet for those, such as I, who know little what it means to be sickly, it is natural to pay little mind to the great fortune of good health; for health means precisely that one need not be concerned with the body, which, in a synthetic relationship with consciousness, allows us to go beyond it for a purpose, rather than having to make it the end. (Obviously, when I suggest that to be unduly preoccupied with signs of illness is a kind of illness itself, I do not question the wisdom of tests such as mammograms and other means by which we can today practice preventive medicine.)

The good life of the mind . . . the good life of the body. What about the heart? I would be the last to disdain it—although, in truth, separating out these three as though they were not connected is to ignore their synthetic unity. Others have written more eloquently than I could on friendship; again, one thinks of Montaigne, who was aided perhaps in his cultivation of *l'amitié* by his relegation of sexual love to an inferior position, but whose exemplary friendship with La Boétie can be explained chiefly by his phrase, "Because it was he, because it was I." For, to be lasting and preeminent, friendship seems to require the dimension of the unexplainable, that is, what goes beyond the obvious reasons for affection and understanding and involves the ultimately irrational and irreducible self. The same is true for love, an experience so celebrated, from Catullus to Louis Aragon (and damned also—let us not forget Proust, and he is not the severest critic) that it would be foolhardy to dare offer new generalities on the topic. But I cannot pass over entirely the question of human relationships, under penalty of appearing indifferent to the role others play in forming and fulfilling ourselves.

Psychologists and philosophers, including Nietzsche, Lacan, Sartre, and Buber, have insisted on the awakening and mediating role of others. Nietzsche, we all know, asserts that the superior individual must raise himself above others, denying their rights on him. For Lacan, the mirror stage is a disturbing one, for it marks the transition from absolute to contingent, as the self discovers the existence of others and its dependence upon them. For Sartre, the self is always mediated through others, with whom the usual relationship is either sadistic (subordinate the other to oneself) or masochistic (enslave oneself to the other). To seek approval, that is, to attempt to conceal to oneself one's nothingness through receiving ratification from the outside, is bad faith, ontologically and ethically blameworthy. Buber, on the contrary, makes the I-thou relationship both central and authentic.

Does Buber's view correspond better to psychological and moral reality—things as they are and as they should be? It is impossible for me to say; but, in the late twentieth century, we certainly cannot subscribe to the implications of Nietzsche's philosophy, and Sartre's view is a dead end. (Anyhow, he himself lived and thought through others, who to a great extent were the condition of the experiences and reflections that led him to his conclusions.) In any case, the thought of denying value to relationships with those I love, with the purpose of heightening my own value, strikes me as grotesque. To those who created or chose me, my debt is enormous; to those whom I have chosen or created, it is no less substantial and real. If the self is mediated through others, so be it; the relationship is certainly reciprocal, and most human beings find it rewarding, whether they believe in its Christian foundation or not.

"Count no man happy until he dies" was the wisdom of the Greeks, who were, properly, cautious; Oedipus is there, along with Agamemnon, to warn us, and the example of Socrates himself, the philosopher of the life well lived, can be taken to illustrate the ruination of that life—although its other possibility is as an illustration of the way death acquires meaning. Gide, on the other hand, makes his Theseus say in his maturity, "I have done my work; I have lived"—the implication being that the man has accomplished something whose worth remains and that, moreover, the accomplishment has made the man, who is identical to that life.

At what point does this synthetic unity between the life and the work coalesce sufficiently to be discernable? One could argue that it is visible even in the young; for families who have lost a child, that child is loved and remembered *in* and *through* his play, his schooling, his little creations of art or writing or building. But it is most noticeable in those of mature years, like Theseus, for whom the question of happiness has been answered, perhaps not by great happiness itself (as he might have conceived it, younger) but by a replacing of that goal by will directed toward ends he has acknowledged as his, and toward whose realization his life has been instrumental. One does not have to be Theseus to achieve this sense of a life well directed toward its ends, hence properly lived. My cousin Beth, who served in Europe as a nurse in World War II, lost the man she loved to that war; but, after pursuing her profession for some years, she married at last and raised four children. When she said to me some years ago, "My life has been good," she could speak truly; no matter that the illness and death of her husband, and her own decline, awaited her. Even Oedipus concluded, in *Oedipus at Colonus,* that all was well.

Winter Light

*I*n moving pages devoted to his mother's portrait, the narrator of *Remembrance of Things Past* tells how, after his grandmother's death, his mother came to resemble the latter so greatly in appearance, manner, and character that he sometimes mistook her for a moment. This is the handiwork of time, to be sure, but also of a conscious choice to model herself on the revered, departed figure. So it is with me and my parents, since their death, but so also, I sometimes think, with my grandfather, whose heir I feel, or wish, myself to be. Through him I am in touch with the nineteenth century; in me, certain of his habits of life and mind—accumulation of learning, voluminous note-taking, production of books, intellectual independence, regularity of routine combined with love of travel—are still in effect, and, God willing, I shall enter the twenty-first century with them.

In 1933, the year my parents were married, Edward Curtis Hill turned seventy and retired from the full-time practice of medicine. He retained, however, a number of patients, whom he saw in the dining room of the big house on Alameda Avenue in Denver. They came until the early 1940s, when the family moved to Seventh Avenue at Josephine Street. When Grandfather was closeted with one of them, I was admonished to be quiet and go around through the double parlors—territory otherwise off-limits except for family dinners—to get to the kitchen, where my grandmother might be preparing something, or supervising the work of the Irish washerwoman—first a Mrs. Kenyon, then a Mrs. McCullough. This was usually in the afternoon, since for nearly two decades Grandfather continued in the mornings to take the streetcar (later the trolleybus) downtown, where he visited Daniels and Fisher's department store (where he was well known), book dealers and music stores, and Baur's or Russell Stover's candy shops (the latter at least once a week). There would be, however, long

periods when he was away, for he and Grandmother took extensive trips, as I recounted earlier, one around the world in 1937–
1938 and another around the African continent. What those old
women who relied on him did then I cannot say—probably just
waited it out.

Born the year after Grandfather's retirement, I was his sixth and
last grandchild. A snapshot of the period shows me in his arms in
the garden—his hair white, his forehead high and broad, revealing
his impressive cranial capacity; we make one shadow. Since for
many years my parents and I lived within a few blocks of my
grandparents' house—and after we moved to Texas we spent parts
of each summer with them—he was a central figure in my youth;
doubtless it is thanks to him and Grandmother that I have always
felt comfortable around the old, and venerate them to this day.
When I was a child, the books he gave me constituted a good core
library in science and history. During the lean college and graduate
school years, he was generous with me; a $1,000 bond bought at
my birth came due, and he gave me checks that were large for the
time—$50 to buy clothes one year, with the observation that
"'twere better to be dead than out of fashion." When he died in
1958, approaching his ninety-fifth birthday, I was in France.

Born in Cleveland, Illinois, he had gone to Colorado as a young
man (1885) with his mother, sister, and brother. In Saguache, on
the Western Slope, he became involved in politics and edited the
Saguache *Sentinel,* which he co-published with his brother Al. As
he wrote in 1933 from the Gunter Hotel in San Antonio, in reply
to a letter from my father saying that he wanted to get married,
the paper was "a moderate financial success for about a year,
when the brakes were reversed by the election of Ben Harrison,
and the land-office business, previously published by good democrats (and the only important source of income, being $5 each),
was handed over to hungry republicans such as my bow-legged
opponent 'Colonel' Mingay." Apparently the enterprise went under, and Grandfather was cured of his impulse to become involved
in business. But the time in Saguache proved momentous. I quote
from the same letter: "In the meanwhile, fortunately, through my
connection with the Methodist choir, I became acquainted with,

and in due time engaged to, a certain Miss Phoebe Elliott, who advised me to become a physician—an idea that had never entered my head before. So, when, at your present age, I was defeated (as nearly all democrats were then) running for the office of county superintendent of public instruction, I left for Denver to study medicine, having approximately $40 in my pocket."

Grandfather's point was that he and Miss Elliott, who had thick black hair, blue eyes, and pure Celtic blood, did not marry for some time. First, he had to complete his studies and become established. While still a student, he passed his state pharmacy board examinations and became, as he put it, "superintendent of the long-defunct Colorado Women's and Children's Hospital, getting my board and room and the munificent salary of $10 per month (later $20)—and was very happy, as my work pleased me and I got a letter from Miss Phoebe Elliott at least once a week." After his graduation in 1891 from the Gross Medical College—with a $50 prize from a Dr. Buchtel—he was thrown out on his own resources by the closing of the hospital; he fell ill from erysipelas (a predisposing cause being partial starvation).

Fortunately, Miss Elliott and her mother moved to Denver and took him in as a boarder for $2 a week. He began to get some medical work—mostly obstetric—and cheap insurance examinations at fifty cents or a dollar each; he also did laboratory work and made money by writing. As he told my father, his motto, with respect to marriage, was "Work and Wait." Engaged from the last of June, 1889, he and Phoebe did not marry until May, 1893. My cousin John believed that Phoebe had considerable resources of her own, from her deceased riverboat-captain father in Montreal and prosperous merchant forebears; perhaps so. But a man could not honorably dip into a woman's purse, that is, as Grandfather put it, become a "squaw man." Their marriage lasted nearly sixty years. My elder aunt was born in 1894; five other children followed. Grandfather sent all six of them through the University of Denver, and nearly all pursued professional studies or postgraduate work, at one time or another. He must have worked very hard for decades. For her part, my grandmother bore and raised the children, instructed them at home (only my father,

132

the youngest, attended elementary school), taught the girls to play the piano, traveled to Montreal and elsewhere, with Grandfather or one or more children, and remained as devoted to her native Canada and its ways as she was to her family.

Despite what must have been difficult times in the early years, Grandfather practiced charity from the outset—a custom that to-day's physicians, attached to groups and hospitals and mostly to lucre, would consider out of the question. The most striking case involved a young woman from the East. The daughter of very prosperous people, she had displeased her father by marrying a man of whom he could not approve; he had disowned her. The young couple had come to Colorado, where they hoped to make money off mining claims. Even during bitter winters, they lived for some years in a tent in the foothills. Without charge, Grand-father took care of her and particularly of him, a sickly man, not meant for the harsh life of a miner. Their infants all died, and the man himself did not live long. Meanwhile, the wealthy parents departed this life, leaving their fortune to another daughter; when she in turn died, without heirs, it reverted to the sister in Colo-rado, who became a wealthy woman. At her death, she left to my grandfather her entire fortune: a large house, handsome furnish-ings, silver. I have some of the furniture—two chairs covered in horsehair velours, and a mirror table that was made in Europe and shipped up the Mississippi River and then overland.

My grandfather had a gargantuan appetite for learning, with a curiosity and catholicity that strike me as nineteenth-century. He was interested in all sorts of things, principally scientific, but also literary and artistic. His publications include a massive chemistry textbook and a small handbook on popular science. He collected botanical specimens from every continent he visited and especially from the Rockies, concerning whose flora his learning was consid-erable; similarly, he had his own collection of minerals, incorpo-rating many samples obtained through dealers but built around his own gleanings in Colorado. He had butterflies mounted in cases and rows and rows of bottles filled with chemical solutions and medicines. From the time of the early Victrolas, he gathered a good library of recorded music, to which he listened religiously.

Chiefly he had books. When, in 1986, what remained of his library was divided and disposed of, after the death of his spinster daughters, there were over five thousand volumes to deal with; hundreds, nay thousands had been given away previously, to his children and grandchildren. We—each of the surviving grandchildren—took what we wanted, though I could not keep many, having a houseful and an officeful of books already. (The greater part of the five thousand went to Regis College library.) He bought books and magazines from dealers and publishers all over the country and subscribed to or purchased as a lot such series as "The World's Greatest Authors," "A Library of Half-Hours with the World's Greatest Authors," and "The Bibelot." For his own purposes, he took copious notes, typing on an old Underwood; I have a number of his looseleaf notebooks filled with alphabetically arranged information on a wide range of topics—biography, U.S. history, agriculture, pharmacology, paleontology and geology, and religion. The time came, apparently after 1953, when he could no longer type with ease; he then filed handwritten notes, some with a shaky penmanship, in an accordion-style alphabetizer. His tastes in literature and poetry were good, although of course colored by his nineteenth-century education; he quoted with ease from such as Shakespeare and Longfellow. A book by some modern poet—I have now forgotten who—that he read and passed on to me bore, in addition to the date of reading (like all his volumes), the well-deserved remark, "Pretty poor stuff."

Of course it was in medicine and science in general that his knowledge was most authoritative and extensive; he taught chemistry at both the University of Colorado (school of medicine) and the Colorado College of Dental Surgery, and did considerable research in his laboratory. With respect to the practice of medicine, he amassed a vast knowledge, supplemented by wisdom and judgment. My cousin John, himself a physician, believed that Grandfather's acumen was such that even now, with advances in pharmaceuticals and treatments, it could scarcely be improved upon in certain areas. He could not, however, make his youngest son into a strong man. If, in my poetry, there is often a privileging of the body, it is perhaps not only because I am a woman but also because of this family predisposition to give to the body its full due, as the seat and instrument of our affective and intellectual life. A letter from him, dated 1955, as I was about to embark on graduate studies, urges me "not to neglect the measures needed to keep you in prime physical condition."

Many men of the nineteenth century were severe figures of authority. My father considered his father to be a hard man, I believe. There must have been good reason for such a judgment. A razor strop hung in the bathroom; my understanding is that it had been used more than once on bare flesh. Grandfather was perhaps too active in directing his sons toward their careers—at one point he wished for my father to become a dentist—and he may have had little enthusiasm for the woman his son Jack married (he would not have been far wrong; Jack chose her after her sister refused him, and such a choice would be considered auspicious by few). Some oblique comments overheard in my childhood implied also that Grandfather raised obstacles that prevented his daughters from marrying—although letters found after my aunt Mary's death suggest that she remained a spinster perhaps because her affection for a certain James in Canada had been unrequited; and as for my delightful aunt Flora, she had at least one proposal of marriage, which she turned down for her own reasons, if one is to believe letters. Grandfather let the girls leave home to take jobs and do postgraduate work—one attended the University of Michigan and worked in California, another taught in various Colorado towns and went to France. Whatever the case concerning them, the evidence I have is that Grandfather showed patience and understanding toward his youngest son. In the letter from San Antonio, he writes: "I suppose love is an illusion (like friendship, patriotism, etc.), but perhaps our illusions are all that make life worth living. There is no doubt that Della [who became my mother] is a fine, competent girl of high character, and if anything will make a *real man* of a man, it is the true love for and from a worthy woman." But he added: "The next and most difficult thing is to make yourself worthy of her." A sequel to this letter explains what he meant. My poor father was apparently not only about to marry but also contemplating a business arrangement, in partnership with a friend, which, if he signed it, would lead him to abandon his plans to become certified as a teacher. (The proposed undertaking seems not to have been his failed venture as a grocer, which cast a cloud over some of my childhood, but rather a drugstore.) Writing this time from the Hotel McAllister in Miami, Grandfather replied thus:

> I think it is best for you to *finish* with the term of preparation for teaching, so that you might get, at least at first, substitute work as a teacher in Denver. There is always satisfaction in finishing anything, and business opportunities at the present time which require money are apt to improve by waiting and not being too eager to accept them.
>
> In favor of the idea is, as you say, being to a considerable degree independent (even a teacher has sometimes to be a politician) and doing regular work that one likes to do, providing you do like such work. Against the proposition are the following facts: a rather poor corner only four blocks from two established drugstores [probably those at the corner of Alameda and Downing]; very long hours . . . ; a penny-watching business, for which you may or may not be adapted; in other words, a special aptitude for a small business, which you may or may not have. [He did not.] Partnerships are in general undesirable.

Grandfather added that "the Hills have not been a shining success in business. My father failed as a small merchant during the panic of 1857. My partnership with the physician in the drug store (too much in his favor) . . . yielded only enough to keep my mother, my sister and myself and two or three nieces during the time when we had a bad renter on the farm." (This must have been in Illinois.) "In partnership with my brother Al in the newspaper, I yielded, as often, to a rather foolish generosity and virtually gave him my share of the newspaper plant." Despite all this, Grandfather agreed, upon his return home, to hand over to my father $1,000 of the money that would be his, providing—and this is a very significant proviso, showing sense and sensitivity—"it is the wish and will of *your mother* and *your fiancee.*" What happened to this drugstore business—if indeed it was that—I do not know. My heart aches at the thought of the anxieties my poor father must have gone through in this connection; even more than other Hills, he was ill-adapted for business of any sort, being even more generous, foolish even, incapable of creating in himself the commercial mentality.

In any case, in these remarks on marriage, career, and business, I see my grandfather's wisdom and love for his son, and also something of his own failures—a side of him that is much less visible in the botanical notebooks and typed pages that speak to me of his intellectual interests, a side I need to know if I am to understand him fully as a mortal and see myself as his descendant. He must have suffered greatly when Jack died at sea in the Battle of Leyte Gulf; a parent does not like to survive his son nor think of his prolonged suffering. His letter to us in Texas was understated: "It is very sad to think that we shall never see his smile or hear his voice again." He then grieved when Phoebe died in 1952; but this loss was more predictable, for, short of an accident that kills both together, every spouse can expect either to predecease the other—and know in advance what grief he is leaving—or to remain himself after the other goes.

Grandfather's old age had, nevertheless, a serene aspect. After he ceased seeing patients and then going downtown by himself—he was taken in by an unscrupulous haberdashery salesman one day, who sold him a zoot suit, and then he had a fall on Sixteenth Street—he spent almost all his time in his sunroom study or his basement work area, coming out for lunch, then dinner. After dinner he often continued reading in bed. Assisted by his son Kenneth, he acted as his own physician, and for his weakening heart took strong coffee and digitalis. On occasion he took a little wine, although he had voted for prohibition, my father told me, because he wanted to set a proper example for his offspring. He enjoyed taking his family out to eat, at favorite restaurants, including the Brown Palace Hotel. As his appetite declined, the portions seemed to expand: once, at a roadside restaurant in Wyoming, he was given such a huge salad that he politely asked the waitress,

"What am I supposed to do with this?" At age eighty-nine, he was honored by the Denver Medical Society as the oldest of its fifty-year veterans. He had always loved drives to the mountains, but finally had to give up crossing Berthoud and the other high passes to the west; instead, my aunt Flora would take him to Colorado Springs or north to Fort Collins and Laramie, which is higher than Denver and cooler in the summer but is accessible over gentler passes. (He had never learned to drive, but the "girls" drove from an early age and there was always a big car—Buick, Packard, or De Soto—in the garage.) After I learned to drive, I was sometimes instructed to take him out for a little turn around the neighborhood or to a park.

When, early in 1957, he was having a very irregular pulse and felt that he would not last much longer, he made arrangements for his own cremation and division of his capital among his surviving children. (He did not leave great wealth, since most of his money was invested in lifetime annuities—not a good bargain for the insurance companies.) In truth, he lived for sixteen more months. The last letter I have of his informs my father of what money will be his, and adds, "Wishing you both a long life and a happy one." His companions in those last years were a parakeet named Timmie and my aunt Flora, who took care of him with great devotion, coming home during her lunch hour to prepare his meal and assist him in any way possible. Since all days finally come, both of joy and of sorrow, at last his heart gave out. Perhaps he would have agreed with what Brillat-Savarin's mother is said, in her extreme old age, to have told her son: "When you reach my age, you will understand that death, like sleep, is a need."

I knew my grandfather only in the winter of his life. This should make me melancholy, and does (and anyway, I am greatly given to hibernal depression). And yet I connect his winter with light—the soft, cheerful rays of a late November afternoon, breaking through the clouds to the southwest. "More light!" said the aged Goethe; Gide, who quoted the phrase, added on his deathbed that it was always the struggle between what is reasonable and what is not, leaving it to his witnesses and heirs to argue whether the reasonable or the unreasonable was closer to the light. (One thinks of the parallel development, during the eighteenth century, of both the rationalistic Enlightenment and that other, antirational appeal to the light, Illuminism.) From Grandfather, I retain some of the books, the notebooks, the example; John took his glass-front bookcases and medical instruments, which he displayed in his office; Grandfather's descendants, numerous by now, all have his genes. And I have many photographs of him, including snap-shots from a trip to Wyoming, passport pictures, a studio portrait, and—one of my favorites—a sepia-toned photograph taken with a wide-angle lens at Mesa Verde, where he sits, dressed in a suit and cap—the lone living person visible among the ruins that the Anasazi abandoned centuries ago. In the stark visual confrontation of two epochs, two civilizations, I read much of the American drama, one that appears in my poetry and has not ceased to pre-occupy me, and with respect to which he serves as intermediary for me. And as I study the photograph, there is another confron-tation, not only between generations, but between my present and my own history, which Grandfather represents. For he too now is the past, which, like the stone at Mesa Verde, smooth and yellow, casts on us the pale, reflective light of wintertime.

"Turn My Face Out to the West"

*I*nside my sleeping bag—or rather, inside my *two* sleeping bags, one within the other, and still barely enough for my old bones and blood, thinned by years in the South—I slide down deeper, my head entirely covered now, and only my mouth, at the side opening, in touch with the cool air. I adjust my pajama collar to cover my neck as well as possible; a wool scarf would be nice, but might strangle me in the night. Despite these precautions, a shiver sneaks down my spine. The night *is* cold: rain came at sundown, and we are high in the Sangre de Cristos. But the shiver is not just from the mountain chill, I think. After nearly thirty years, an old feeling has revived, as if the body had its own memory, unleashed by the stillness of the forest, the feel of pine needles under me, the smell of damp ponderosa and willows from the meadow and the lingering smoke from the fire, over which earlier we cooked pork cutlets and asparagus and which now is reduced to coals. The stars are just now starting to cut through the clouds with their diamond bits; at the coldest part of the night, when the silence intensifies so that it presses through to the mind, they will be out in full numbers, the bright Big Dipper leading them on.

The feeling is not, however, only of the body; it is a metaphysical shiver, one that goes beyond the five senses and the powers of the rational mind. I believe what I can: I do not believe that God is walking in the mist across the meadow, or moving through the pines that reach up the mountain into the night—though if He were, surely the shred of spirit that is somehow married to our muscles and organs would recognize its Source in a shiver of ecstasy. The sensation is not a Proustian recognition or an ordinary experience of déjà vu, and it cannot be localized in any particular recollection—although I have a rich store of memories of sleeping out in the Rockies during my girlhood and even in my twenties. (I can even include a few episodes of camping later in the Blue

Ridge in Virginia, although—was it a question of altitude, of air or flora, of a state of mind?—the feeling was not quite the same.) Neither, despite being connected to my childhood, is this experience an emotional replaying of some crucial experience or trauma. Nor is it identical to an esthetic feeling—although my admiration has been stirred by the vastness and beauty of the sagebrush desert that we crossed earlier in the day, a shimmering peacock tail of turquoise blue and soft dusty green and the bright oranges and yellows of sunlight; stirred, too, by the mountain range that for hours, a shadowy keel, ploughed the blue horizon ahead of us, but which we finally overtook in all its majesty, and on whose dark green flanks we now repose. The sensation has, mysteriously, an element of the sacred. It is most like a vision, where one sees differently, as though from a great distance . . .

Being in the mountains again, camping out in territory that I knew as a girl and young woman, is a matter partly of choice, partly of chance. (My reasons for the choice will be clear shortly. I will seize this occasion to deny that the concept of the unconscious will illuminate them. Let Dr. Freud say what he will: since his system is based on the reduction of behavior to a few basic, universal impulses, all the analysis in the world of tree and mountain imagery—I have deliberately named objects with sexual shapes—will never explain why a particular person finds meaning in such settings or imagery, why one prefers pines, another oaks, one broad valleys, another the verticality of peaks. This is not the only reason why I reject his understanding of human behavior, but it would suffice.) The previous summer, my daughter and I went to France. This June, she is taking a summer course at Tulane; I have just finished an enormous research project and need some relaxation; my husband, not much of a traveler, as I have observed before, is happy to keep house with her. So I have left for ten days, going first to Chicago, to meet my cousin John, then, with him, to Colorado Springs, where we have visited with my cousin Beth Ann, and now in New Mexico, where four of us—descendants of my grandfather Hill—have decided to meet. "Why not go camping?" someone suggested earlier. We have picked out our spots—yesterday, Chaco Canyon, so difficult of access; today, Jemez State

Monument, near some fine petroglyphs, in the Santa Fe National Forest; and, tomorrow, Bottomless Lakes. Inexplicably, John forgot his tent—packing only the poles—so we have no canvas between us and the sky and ground. But the rain was brief, we have eaten well and drunk a little wine, and we are comfortable on a bed of earth. The trip will be so enjoyable, the four of us such happy campers, that we will do it again the following year, sleeping out at various sites in the canyon country in northeastern Arizona and then near the Navajo Reservoir.

Perhaps camping out here means different things to us. Edith knows New Mexico best; she has lived here for nearly twenty years, and she and her husband are very knowledgeable about Indian ruins and artifacts. She is not a rugged person, but is a willing camper, accustomed to sleeping out on harsh terrain, which she loves as home. Jean, who lives in Tabernash, Colorado, has always been a mountain girl, and is never so happy as when she is camping and hiking—which she does often and vigorously, at nearly sixty. John—well, he is game for anything, loving life, full of energy, and able to hike down steep trails, despite his bad knee and portly figure. I—I love the outdoors in general, especially the West, from which circumstances have separated me and for which I have dreadful longings that no amount of city skyscape can satisfy. (Only the ocean has meant so much to me.) And the history that we find in the Anasazi ruins and various petroglyphs (which I have visited only briefly before) is, to my mind, something of my own history, though it is strange: not without effect does one share the heritage of living under the Western skies.

Unless one is a professional historian, one can scarcely write about American Indians now without feeling foolish and, to some degree, guilty. Perhaps the change in attitude is a healthy one, although I am not sure it will truly help those in whose name it has been imposed. With respect to the Anasazi, at least, we are all in the same position—ignorance; for that canyon-dwelling people disappeared roughly a thousand years ago, and probably has no present-day heirs (although some ethnographers have connected them to the Hopi, and others to the Pueblo Indians). Thus I can claim them as rightfully as anyone, admiring their architectural achievements, their solar-based science, their spirituality, their apparent gentleness, their measures to conserve rain runoff; suffering with them in imagination as they struggled to survive, in a terrain and climate where nature was chary of her gift of water. "And they shall be like trees planted by rivers of water." To one from the arid West, among the most meaningful of scriptural images— never known to the Anasazi—are those of springs and rivers.

Although I am not connected to them except by having been born in this region, I want to say a word also about the Pueblo Indians, some of whose communities the four of us have visited on this trip and who are another focus of my interest in the West. Their culture is a rich mixture of native and Spanish beliefs and customs, now existing beside the industrial and technological civilization of the late twentieth century. In Taos Pueblo, the only remaining example of traditional pueblo architecture, no electricity or gas is used; but many community members live outside the pueblo unit, along the roads leading to town; and there, of course, they have modern conveniences. In the church of San Geronimo, the Taos Indians keep with faithfulness the Catholic ritual, in its peculiarly Hispanic version, giving great importance to such ceremonies as the Christmas Eve procession and the penitential rites; but at their tribal gatherings, such as the big July pow-wow, they engage in dances and ceremonies that go back to pre-Spanish times. The church itself combines pueblo architecture with the Spanish mission style, its icons—the *retablos*—lovely examples of folk art. Their handicrafts incorporate Indian motifs and emblems—connected to the natural world of sun and mountain and rain—mixed with Spanish ones. They share much with their non-Indian neighbors and visitors, but not everything. Similarly, at Jemez and other pueblos where we have stopped, the tribes preserve such traditions as the Cloud Dance, the Deer and the Buffalo Dances, products of another world to which, consciously, they are attempting to preserve their connection, while opening their communal existence to educational and economic developments that they deem necessary. An unusual case of cross-cultural influence, one might say; but it reminds us that we are all products of mixed cultures.

If I wish to reclaim this heritage as partly mine, by choice, I have to acknowledge also the other sides of the West—even if, again, my ancestors were not directly connected to them. To the harshness of nature, in her extremes of cold and heat, in her droughts and winds and snows, in the obstacles raised to man's comfort and survival, was added so much human brutality— sometimes gratuitous and sadistic, often the product of greed, or springing from the struggle to survive or to impose a manner of living—that reading the history of the great movement west is painful indeed. Cannibalism, mass slaughter of people and animals, gang rapes, torture and mutilation, summary injustices, senseless suffering—these mark the opening and development of the West, the change of culture from that of the Plains and Pueblo Indians to that of the Spanish- and English-speaking whites. Unhappily, as a student of European history, I have to acknowledge that this brutality, if exercised in a somewhat wider area in America, is the same that marked the clashes of religious and political powers in the Mediterranean basin and Europe in the millenia preceding the whites' arrival in the New World; to conquer or be conquered, exploit or be exploited was the rule for so many. Small consolation; but it allows me to turn my face again to the West with love, just as I can admire the cathedral of Notre-Dame, the basilica of Vézelay, while knowing that crusaders left from Vézelay to go exterminate the heathen, and that in 1579 the river Seine ran red with the blood of Protestants slaughtered by adherents of the same Catholic faith that had inspired such lofty monuments.

Who among us can escape from such history? Let those rejoice who believe their past includes none of it. Meanwhile, the rest of us must acknowledge what we have come from, while—and this is the wonder of human freedom—dissociating ourselves from what we see as immoral in that past, and in our present. So I look to the West to see what, of its history and culture, should be preserved. There is so much that is good and beautiful: the courage (it was abundant), the independent spirit, combined with a sense of community, the belief in hard work, the love for the land. These are often considered American values in general: in New

England, the Midwest, the South, one would find ready approval of them, and they permeate our literature; but they are more recently, and perhaps more integrally, associated with the West. I see them in my grandparents, who came to Colorado for different reasons, in most of their descendants, through my generation, in the outdoorsmen I knew as a girl, and in many who now make their home in the Rocky Mountain states.

One value in particular is common to present-day Native Americans and the Anasazi (to judge by their ruins), to the girl that I was and remain, and to one of the best strains of modern thought—a value to which both traditional conservatives and contemporary liberals can subscribe. That it presently goes under the unwieldy term of *environmentalism* is only a minor flaw; it is identical to the commitment of many long since dead to preserve their land. How necessary a new ecological economy is should be obvious to almost everyone in the developed nations. Because of the traditions I have alluded to above, its necessity is particularly clear to those in the West. The country itself begs for conservation, for the vastness of the mountains and deserts of the West is deceptive; the country is fragile, its inhabitants vulnerable.

Fragile, those piles of rock, those expanses of sand, sagebrush, and cactus? Yes. Consider the number of years—decades, rather—it takes for reforestation of mountain slopes denuded by forest fires or excessive lumbering; consider the damage done by a desert whirlwind or a swollen creek on a dry range that sheds the rain like oilcloth; think of the delicate balance of vegetable and animal life in the desert and the high elevations, of the vulnerability of deer and elk to the vicious blizzards of mountains and open range. Think, too, of the years required for trash thrown in the forest to decompose, of the near-permanent blight created by strip mining. Thank God at least that in some areas such human abuse has remained relatively limited in scope. The scarcity of water has protected much of the West against overexploitation and overpopulation; my father often remarked that the Big Bend country was saved by its aridity. Unfortunately, water management in the form of dams has created what might once have been called oases but what have turned out to be among the most god-awful products of America—the sprawling, water-guzzling agglomerations of Las Vegas, Phoenix, and their suburbs being among the worst. These urban monstrosities—and similarly Los Angeles and Denver, to a considerable degree—are living off, often squandering, water that belongs, if not to the *people* of the Western Slope of Colorado and Northern California, at least to their plants and animals.

I am aware that vast agricultural areas in California, Arizona, and New Mexico also are irrigated by the dammed waters of the Rio Grande and the Colorado, and that we all consume produce from these areas. But that is not the only way in which we could be fed. The consequent establishment of huge corporate farms (not confined to these states, of course) is not a happy development, nor is the shipping around the country, during all months of the year, of pale, tasteless produce that gives only the appearance of quality. Better a tasty and nutritious tomato in season than pithy, juiceless ones year-round. But in truth it is much more the city residents to whose appropriation of water I object. Boasting often of creating a "desert environment" around their domiciles, the prosperous residents of Sun City and so on have built large houses much bigger than their needs, added paved roads and driveways that create additional water loss through runoff, and planted large lawns of a grass not at all suited for the climate, grass which is as thirsty as if it were back in Kentucky; and when water rationing is established, they object and demand more still from the northern mountains. And the bankers and developers prosper ever, like the wicked mentioned in the Bible.

So much for water and its misuse. I could preach, too, on strip mining and air pollution—the huge Navajo coal mine and Four Corners Power Plant, disfiguring the land and poisoning the skies so that residents of Phoenix can squander electricity—and the dreadful highway billboards that are so much more offensive in God's desert than along a turnpike in New York; and then there is trash, to which I referred earlier. When we broke camp, we left no waste of any sort except bits of charcoal and ashes; I confess that they are a small eyesore, and we probably should have removed them, especially since it takes decades for charcoal to disintegrate. So in that respect we too were polluters, despite our concern for preserving our surroundings. And of course we burned gasoline to get there and back. The lesson is that human beings cannot exist on the earth without leaving some mark; we violate the atmosphere and the surface of the planet by our very existence. At one time, theological doctrine was such that what I have called "violation" was considered a duty: man is supposed to have been given dominion over the beasts of the air and the field, over the earth itself, whose fruits he was to harvest, all *ad majorem Dei gloriam*. To what excesses of ugliness and destruction, indeed of endangerment, not to mention the suffering of sentient creatures, such dominion can lead is all too clear now. If we have a duty, it is to cease our gross abuse of the planet and its creatures, through containing our desires and practicing an economy of soil, air, and water that will restore some of the freshness of the earth and preserve it not only for our descendants but for its own sake.

That this economy must be balanced against the legitimate needs of human beings not only to eat and drink but to develop their minds and bodies I do not dispute. Nature herself is a rough, sometimes a fine, balance; we will be true to our natural condition if we achieve such equilibrium between ourselves and our environment. Let me not hear that this will ruin our national economy. The economy can be built around restoring the land as well as on gouging it; technology, that sorcerer's apprentice, surely can be disciplined to undo some of its mistakes. Such technological, social, and moral matters should keep our best thinkers busy for several generations, if their attention is not entirely consumed by racial and ethnic quarrels, food supply problems, and localized wars.

This concern, I have said, can bring together conservative and liberal, the Western rancher and the city dweller from the East. Some schools of thought now trace environmentalism to various philosophers, including, amazingly, Heidegger. I have no objection to that, but believe that the full sense of what raping the landscape means is most fully available to the observer who sees damage done to a range or a river that he loves. Unfortunately, even in the West, where there are so many people engaged in protecting the land, the exploiters, or just the careless and indifferent, remain more numerous.

I began this essay by identifying an experience I called metaphysical, and here I have devoted several pages to what is clearly the physical. But the former has always been rooted in the latter: we have no way of going beyond ourselves other than using our own selves, as even the greatest mystics and saints would acknowledge. I return to the Anasazi, whose spiritual life—to judge by the position and design of the kivas and by other facts that reveal something about their ceremonies—was closely associated with the movement of the sun, on the one hand, and the physical existence of the community members on the other—the two connected, of course, since the solar year marked the seasons for growing corn and hunting and, by analogy, the spring, summer, autumn, and winter of human life. The Anasazi probably would not even have understood the distinction between earth as *fact* and earth as *meaning*. That in the silence of the forest, which I loved as a girl, and in the dark of the night, spread out on the earth, which is our nourisher and our final destination, I should feel in touch with something that I am, or was, and yet seems to go beyond the rational either bespeaks the power of self-delusion in even those with trained minds, or reveals that tellurian force still present and available to us, to which we have been invited by the high mesas, the sea of wild grasses and sage, and the guardian peaks that are in touch with the heavens.

What I have had, I believe, is an intimation of *order*. Notwithstanding theories of physics that emphasize randomness, and the strain of epistemological thought that insists that categories come from us, not from the world, I find order in nature—or at least I deem it more reasonable, more fruitful to see it there; and to suppose that nature in its turn reveals another order is consistent with the relationship between our mind and the world, of which it is both container and contained. Before the arrival of the Spanish, the Taos Indians, much like the Anasazi and other peoples of the Four Corners area, believed that the Great Spirit dwelt in the mountain, to which the spirits of the deceased repaired, and below which the existence of people, animals, and plants unfolded in an orderly fashion, in accordance with the regular movement of the heavenly bodies. Order above, order below; order in nature, hence in culture, which was the fulfilling on a communal scale of the laws of existence, in imitation (I mean this in the best, fullest sense) of cosmic order. Art certainly, and even language, must have been perceived as connected to this order: pictographs were presumably intended to act on the invisible as well as the visible, and it is hard to imagine ceremonies in which, along with dance, music, and perhaps sacred food and drink, words would not play a role in establishing the connections between the physical life of human beings and the spiritual life to which they would accede.

Of this comprehensive, unbroken sense of order, not everything remains, obviously; I said myself that I did not believe that the spirit of God was walking on the mountain. But much is still accessible to us: the beauty of the hills at morning, of the stark black canyons and the sage flats is still powerfully moving; we continue to desire a sense of community in relationship to the land; and we still look to art and language to tell us who and what we are. Those who would change the world, or themselves—just as difficult—have long gone either to the mountaintop or the desert, to meditate in solitude on the radiance of the light and the splendor of God, the vastness of the earth—mirroring man's desire—and the pettiness of human achievement; John the Baptist and Saint Jerome have modern equivalents in Pierre Jean Jouve, whose devotional poetry is often centered on the desert experience, and—strangely—Camus, with his agnostic meditations. The western wilderness, where a few seers and prophets are still crying to us, gives that same bizarre sense of which Camus speaks in "The Guest," of being the only place where one accustomed to its stones can truly live. I cannot believe that in the order of this landscape there is not an order of the spirit; when I waken later, at the hour of deep silence, after the night has been emptied of everything except cold, still stars, perhaps the words for it will come.